THE WITCH'S MONSTERS BOOK 2

Blood and Malice
The Witch's Monsters, Book Two

Cover design by Luminescence Covers

ISBN-13: 978-1-948455-33-6

ALSO BY SARAH PIPER

Reverse Harem Romance

THE WITCH'S MONSTERS

Blood and Midnight

Blood and Malice

Blood and Madness

TAROT ACADEMY

Spells of Iron and Bone

Spells of Breath and Blade

Spells of Flame and Fury

Spells of Blood and Sorrow

Spells of Mist and Spirit

THE WITCH'S REBELS

Shadow Kissed

Darkness Bound

Demon Sworn

Blood Cursed

Death Untold

Rebel Reborn

M/F Romance

VAMPIRE ROYALS OF NEW YORK

Dorian & Charlotte

Dark Deception

Dark Seduction

Dark Obsession

Gabriel & Jacinda

Heart of Thorns

Heart of Fury

Heart of Flames

1

HUDSON

A dark little whisper nagged inside, making my wings twitch.

Something sure as shit ain't right.

From my perch on the highest turret on the eastern side of Keradoc's castle, I scanned the scene, looking for signs of trouble.

Seemed like the whole of Amaranth City had turned out for the Feast of the Beast, and the few who *hadn't* shown up were most likely out casing houses and apartments, helping themselves to the revelers' unattended loot.

Course, the thieves would most likely be tracked down and murdered within a day, but that was all part of the game. Real entertainment was scarce in Midnight; everyone had to make their own fun.

Bass thumped from the ground floor, the music even louder than the shouts and whoops of the drunken assholes in attendance, all of the noise making the stones beneath my feet vibrate. The place was so packed, half the guests had already been pushed out onto the grounds. Everywhere I looked, people were either fighting or fucking —sometimes both. All around the castle, the ground was muddy with spilled booze and puke and blood. I wondered whose sorry ass would be tasked with tomorrow's cleanup.

Grateful for the relatively fresher air up on the turrets, I took a deep breath and dropped into a glide, circling the perimeter. I spotted three of Keradoc's gargoyle guards making the rounds, but they looked to be about as drunk as the rest of the riffraff and were easily dodged.

Clearly, the warlord needed better security. Not that I was gonna drop *that* little comment in the suggestion box.

Shitty security or not, I wasn't about to let my guard down. Haley was counting on me. All of them were. And that voice inside me wasn't getting any quieter.

Took me a while, but after my fourth loop around the property, I finally spotted them—Saint and Jax following Gem through the melee outside. They weren't looking up at me, though. Too focused on their destination.

The hell they going?

I followed from above as they elbowed their way through the mass of sweaty bodies and headed for a back entrance—kitchens, most likely. Some servant or cook was standing outside the door, but Jax took him out.

Shit.

That whisper inside me grew to a shout. No way would Jax kill some random fae on a whim—not even one of Keradoc's random fae. Way too risky, especially with Haley involved.

I was about to drop down and follow them into whatever shitstorm they were gearing up for, but a new threat buzzed through my blood—sharp and sudden and utterly unmistakable.

Haley. She was in trouble, and fucking scared. Thanks to the bond, her fear was so palpable, it may as well have been my own.

Leaving Jax and Saint to fight their own battles, I zoomed back up toward the fourth level, following the insistent pull of my connection to Haley. The pain. It felt like a fishing line reeling me in, a sharp hook right through the gut.

In seconds, I knew *exactly* where she was.

Throne room. I was intimately familiar with it. Centuries ago, before my life went to shit here and I was relegated to working private security gigs for Midnight's drug and weapons dealers, I was head guardian to one of the Midnight noble families. They spent a lot of time hobnobbing at the castle, kissing the ass of a different ruler while Keradoc was still clawing his way to power. Keradoc was no different though—all them fae fuckers liked to keep my kind close. Gargoyles were better than fae at taking bullets and arrows.

But Haley certainly wasn't there as an ass-kissing noble tonight. Or even as a spy.

She was a prisoner.

I saw her the second the windows came into view, bound to the throne on the dais.

The pain in my gut turned to raw fucking rage.

Hell no, asshole. Wrong fucking night, wrong fucking witch.

I tucked my wings close and arrowed straight for the windows, ready to smash through the glass, grab that purple-eyed fae fucker, and rip the spine from his body. But just before impact, a hot streak sizzled up my spine, tearing through me with an agony that left me gasping for air. My back twisted against the pain as my muscles seized up, sending me into a fucking tailspin.

I crashed to the ground behind the castle like a warplane shot out of the sky, sending up a wave of mud and debris.

My thick hide saved my bones from shattering, but it still fucking hurt like the devil. I had just enough strength to roll onto my back and wipe the muck from my eyes. I wasn't far from where I'd seen Gem take Jax and Saint. The door they'd ducked into was mere feet away.

But it may as well have been a hundred miles for all the time I had to get there.

Before I even fully caught my breath, my attackers were

already swooping down for the kill shot. Dark shapes closed in fast from overhead—fifteen seconds until impact.

Wings. Claws. Horns and fangs.

Fucking gargoyles.

Not the drunk mercs I'd seen earlier, but street fighters. No sense of honor or loyalty among them—and yeah, I was speaking from experience.

Garrison, Draven, and—worst of the lot—Mad Marco, who made up for his lack in stature with balls-out craziness. Three of the six Stone City homegrown assholes who'd slaughtered people I cared about, destroyed my old life in Midnight, and left me for dead.

Twice.

Haley's fear spiked again, sending another zing straight to my gut. Pretty sure the other guys were in deep shit too. I needed to get to them—and fast.

I closed my eyes. Gave myself one more heartbeat to get my lungs working and get my ass out of the dirt.

Rage was the best fuel there was, and between Haley's fear and my old enemies attacking me, I was *furious*. I stoked those flames hard, let them propel me out of the mud and onto my feet. I was still in warrior form, nothing broken far as I could tell, but I wasn't about to give anything away.

Keeping my wings limp and my shoulders hunched, I struck a weak pose as all three of 'em landed and closed ranks around me, claws out and snarls twisting their gruesome faces.

Unlike last time they'd gotten the drop on me, they'd come alone tonight—no dark witch to do their bidding. But whatever they'd hit me with in the sky wasn't gargoyle-made. It was magick. And there was a hundred percent chance they were packin' more, because pricks like them never fought their own battles.

"Look what the cat dragged back from the human realm, boys." Marco started in right away, predictable as fuck. His eyes were wide and crazy, his familiar gap-toothed grin splitting his face—the rare gargoyle who looked the same amount of ugly whether he was a statue or a human. Now, in his warrior form, he shook out his tattered wings and shifted from one foot to the other, twitchy as hell. "Guess your vacation on the other side didn't work out so well."

"Welcome home, motherfucker." This, from Garrison, the biggest and dumbest of the lot. Talked a good game but sucked in a fight.

I pretended to cower in silence, keeping my head low. The closer they got, the less energy I'd have to expend taking them down, and no, that wouldn't hamper my enjoyment of it in the least.

"What's wrong, Hudson?" Marco taunted, tilting his head and peering up at me with those crazy eyes. "After all these centuries, you're still not talking? Not even to your oldest friends?"

Talking? Totally unnecessary, much as he liked to flap his lips. Midnight-bred gargoyles were connected—long as no one was actively shielding, we could tap into one another's minds to communicate. I'd been shielding against every last one of them fuckers since I set foot back in this realm, but now it was time to send out a broadcast.

That you, Marco? Hard to recognize you when you're not cowering behind a witch. Shit, boy. You're a lot shorter than I remember.

"And you're a lot more *alive* than I remember," he sneered. "Guess we'll have to do something about that." He slammed a fist into my gut. I was ready for it though—saw it coming a mile off. I doubled over, feigning pain, and the other two rock-heads pounced on cue.

Yeah. Not happening, fuckholes.

I reared up to my full height and smashed my fists into their faces, sending them both sailing backward through the air. They hit the ground with twin thuds, and I spun around, landing a solid kick to Marco's chest. He stumbled back but didn't go down.

With a fierce growl, he came at me again, slashing his talons across my chest. I dodged the worst of it and ducked low, then plowed into him headlong, taking his ass down.

Set to the soundtrack of the still-thumping party music,

we wrestled on the ground, trading punches and slashes—a blow to the jaw here, a gash along the ribs there. I was bigger and stronger, but that little fucker was fast and wily. One cheap knee-shot to the balls, and he sent me rolling off him, giving him just enough time to scramble back to his feet.

Ignoring the throbbing pain in my groin, I sucked in a breath and rose to face him once more. Garrison and Draven were back in the mix now, all three of the beasts circling me like wild dogs, panting and growling, salivating for a bite. Blood and sweat dripped into my eyes, but I didn't dare blink. Didn't dare give them fuckers a chance to take me out.

Three on one? They probably could've, had they been smarter.

Yet no one made another move.

Whole thing was fucking futile, anyway. Gargoyles in warrior form were nearly impossible to kill—aside from a soft bit of flesh at the throat that could be pierced with a sword or an arrow, we had thick, ultra-protective hides, massive muscles, and we could escape most ground skirmishes by taking flight. Best chance at killing us was to take us by surprise in our human form or get us to turn to stone, then smash us like bad pottery.

But here, tonight?

Without a sunlight spell to turn my ass to stone—or a few sharp weapons and better aim—these fuckers didn't have much of a shot, and they damn well knew it.

Which meant...

Fuck.

They weren't here to take me down. They were just a distraction.

I could still sense Haley, though the signal was getting weaker. I hoped that didn't mean *she* was getting weaker.

"What's wrong?" Marco asked, wiping the blood from his mouth as he leered up at me. "Lose another one of your charges? Guess some things never change."

"Too bad, really," Draven piped in. He licked his lips and grunted. "Such a pretty little witch. I would've loved to have a go at that."

The tremble began in my hands, quickly shooting up my arms and across my back. My muscles tensed for another fight, talons curling, everything inside me eager for a bloodbath.

You're fucking dust, I sent out. *All of you.*

Marco nodded, finally shutting his trap and letting his thoughts come to me instead. *Someday, maybe. But not tonight.*

He raised his arms and pointed something at my chest. A gun, I realized. Manmade. Useless against me.

I spread my arms and smiled, welcoming the nip of those useless little bullets. *Looks like someone's got a new toy. Compensating, maybe?*

You tell me, cocksucker. Marco fired off a whole mess of rounds, the bullets biting into my hide like annoying mosquitos. I plucked one of them from my chest and tossed it at him.

He hit me with one last shot in the gut.

When he was done jerking off his new gun, he stood there watching me expectantly, smoke curling from the end of the barrel.

Yeah, definitely *compensating.* I laughed, inside and out, and stalked toward him, my talons itching for a chance to spill more of his blood. All of it. *Got anything bigger, or is that the best you—*

All at once, my body froze up on me, and a new grin lit up that motherfucker's face.

A dozen tiny explosions tore through my insides, chewing through bone and muscle, unleashing a flood of pure, white-hot agony.

These were no ordinary bullets. None that I'd ever had the fucked-up pleasure of being shot with, anyway—not in the realms of monsters *or* men—which was saying a lot.

Fuck. Me.

I stumbled to my knees as my muscles stiffened. Everything inside me was turning to stone, but not because I'd shifted. Felt like I'd chugged a few hundred gallons of cement.

"Ultraviolet bullets," Marco boasted out loud, admiring his gun. "They ignite on contact—little balls of sunshine packed into a human death machine. Say what you will about dark witches, Hudson, but they really are ingenious bitches when they need to be."

Before I could even ask what constituted a witch's need for ingenuity, he lifted the gun again. Stepped close.

Then he spat in my face like a fucking coward. Jammed the barrel into the spot between my eyes and...

Bang.

My world disappeared.

2

KERADOC

Evander.

The name slipped from the fugitive's lips and right through my defenses, prodding at something that felt like a memory. Images flashed in my mind—a fae child laughing, his silver eyes alight with mischief as he bent his head close to share a secret. A father playfully wrestling with his boys in the soft grass. The scent of sweet cakes cooling on a sill…

Another time, another place. Certainly not mine.

Blinking away the odd images, I stepped down from the dais, leaving the Darkwinter witch bound to the throne behind me.

Still on his knees, the vampire-fae fugitive my guards had captured gazed up at me strangely, his silver eyes so like my real eyes. Similar too were the set of his jaw and the sharpness of his cheekbones, and the grin that tipped higher on one side than the other. It was as if we'd been cast from the very same mold.

But for the glamour I'd been wearing for the last eighteen months, I could've been gazing into a mirror.

"It's really you," he whispered as I approached. Blood leaked from a half-dozen wounds in his chest, hawthorn stakes jutting out at odd angles, sapping his strength. His pain must've been unbearable, yet his eyes held only wonder. Happiness.

Evander...

"No one gave you permission to speak, slave." One of my guards kicked the prisoner in the back, sending him sprawling. He caught himself on his hands with a grunt but made no effort to get back to his knees. A coughing fit seized him, wringing the blood from his lungs out onto the polished floor. The guards had dragged away the remains of the executed shifters but had yet to clean up their mess. Now, it mingled with the blood of my new prisoners in a dark, wet stain. The scent of copper and fear hung heavy in the air.

"Keradoc!" the witch cried out, as fiery as ever. I didn't need to turn around to know she was still struggling against her bonds. "Help him! *Help* him!"

At her desperate cries, the second fugitive—a one-eyed demon shot full of metal bolts—winced, as if the fear in her voice hurt him even more than the devil's trap sigils sucking away his life force.

Even more than watching his mate suffer brutally on the floor beside him.

The vampire-fae lifted his head once more. His arms trembled. Blood leaked from his nose and mouth, but he was still staring at me with awe.

"Do you not remember?" he whispered. "Do you not know your…" His words trailed off into another wet cough that seemed to stretch on for an eternity, but through it all, one word rang out clear, whispered over and over again like a prayer.

Evander. Evander. Evander.

The echo of it unleashed another flicker of images—two fae boys swimming in a cool emerald-green lake, diving for make-believe buried treasure. A mother calling them back to the shore for lunch, the sand pink and glittery beneath her bare toes. The rustle of the breeze through treetops dripping with silver leaves.

An odd warmth spread through my chest, quickly chased by a sucking emptiness so cold it left me gasping.

I cleared my throat and dismissed the visions, reclaiming my focus. This was obviously another of Melantha's games—some wicked spell meant to disarm me and distract me from her machinations with the Darkwinter witch.

No matter. When this war was finally over, I'd make the dark goddess pay. By the time I finished with her, the banishment she was enduring now would look like a pleasant vacation.

"Keradoc," the witch called out again, cutting straight through my thoughts like a blade through flesh.

I turned to her, drawn by the anger in her voice. The righteousness.

The contrast of the raw bones and sharp, polished obsidian of my throne against her soft skin and artfully painted face was so striking, it nearly stole my breath. Death and beauty, darkness and light. Both suited her equally.

A smile touched my lips. For all Melantha's tricks, the blood witch Haley Barnes was *not* a disappointment. Not only was she beautiful, she was sharp-tongued, passionate, clever, and just this side of mad.

Precisely how I needed her.

No witch in her *right* mind would attempt the ancestral ritual required to channel her Darkwinter kin—Midnight's most formidable enemies. Haley herself would certainly refuse at first, but I had no doubts she'd come around soon enough.

Now that I'd captured her companions, persuading her to cooperate would be much easier.

"*Do* something," she implored, and the fire sparking in her green eyes ignited a more recent memory—one I could absolutely claim as my own.

Her lips crashing into mine as she wrapped her legs around me, stealing a kiss that left us both breathless. The feel of her silky hair in my hands as I laid her on the dais and gave her what she seemed to so desperately want...

The taste of her still lingered on my tongue, threatening to make me hard again.

But no. It wasn't me she'd wanted. The witch had seen through my glamour, however briefly, and mistaken me for another.

Her vampire-fae, I realized now. The Midnight fugitive who seemed to be wearing my real face.

More dark magick. More trickery.

My blood simmered as Melantha's betrayal burned through me anew. Was there no spell she wouldn't conjure, no illusion she wouldn't cast in her endless attempts at vengeance?

I clenched my fists and closed my eyes, forcing myself to remain steady. In control. Unraveling in front of my guards and prisoners would put everything at risk, and I'd worked too hard, too tirelessly for that.

"Evander..." the fugitive said once more, his voice a gurgling whisper as he continued to drown in his own blood. New images flashed through my mind—fae children chasing each other through a thick forest. A festival in the heart of the oaken woods, boughs glittering with lights, couples dancing merrily as red and gold leaves fluttered on the breeze like birds...

Behind my eyes, a dull ache throbbed to the beat of an old song lingering on the edge of memory…

“Please, Keradoc.” The witch’s voice cut through the din, chasing away the music and the visions both. When I opened my eyes again, I found her gazing back at me, her face pained.

I climbed back up the dais and approached the throne. “What was that, little thief?”

The demon responded before she could find her words. “Touch her and you’ll—”

One of my guards shot him with another bolt, silencing him.

“I’ll… I’ll do anything you ask of me,” the witch stammered. “Just stop hurting them. Please… please don’t kill them.” Tears brimmed in her eyes, dousing the last of her fire. She was suddenly exhausted and weak.

Pathetic.

Anger stirred inside me. This woman, this formidable witch had traveled to Midnight and risked her life in an attempt to steal my blood. My blood! Even after I’d exposed her lies and taken her prisoner, she’d continued to taunt me, to fight me, to burn with indignation.

Yet now, at the sight of her wounded companions, she crumpled like a flower crushed beneath a soldier’s boot?

Had I been wrong about her mettle? Her power?

“Help them,” she begged again, not meeting my eyes.

I gripped the arms of the throne and bent low, leaning

so close to her the berries-and-cream scent of her skin filled my senses. Ignoring the stirrings of my cock, I said softly, "My apologies, little thief. I can't quite hear you above the pathetic moans of my prisoners. Did you have a request? "

"Yes." She finally glanced up and met my eyes. That old fire blazed anew, and at my answering grin, she flashed one of her own. Sly. Triumphant. *Wicked.* "Get fucked, asshole. You're going *down.*"

3

HALEY

Thanks to Keradoc's obsession with sharp objects—obsidian and bones, in this case—I finally sawed through the fae-spelled ropes and sliced a deep gouge in my palm, coating my ring in fresh blood.

Now, I took more than a little pleasure in watching that smug grin fall off the warlord's face.

"Get fucked, asshole. You're going *down*." I slammed a blood-soaked palm against his chest. Power scorched the air as a blast of magick exploded at my touch, sending him crashing down the dais.

With another quick spell, I called up a magickal barrier around the guys. The guards rushed forward, but it was too late. I leaped from the throne and bolted down the dais, sealing myself inside the barrier with Elian and Jax before Keradoc could bark out an order to attack.

A wall of bright-red magick surged and crackled

around us, enclosing us in a temporary safe haven impervious to weapons and fists.

Finally righting himself, Keradoc commanded the guards to break through, but they were no match for the magickal shield.

"Nice work, angel." Jax managed a thin smile, but he was fading fast. Blood soaked into his shirt around the bolts and leaked from a deep gash on his forehead, sliding into the cavern of his missing eye.

He couldn't even lift a hand to my shoulder without wincing.

"Sit tight," I told him. "We'll figure this out. Just... just give me a minute."

I reached out to touch the barrier. It brightened in response, but just like that night in Blackbone Forest with the raven gryphon, I had no idea how long it would hold.

Didn't matter, though. Five minutes or an hour, eventually it would fizzle out, and we'd have to fight our way out of this room.

I needed to get my men back on their feet.

I dropped down in front of Elian, gently helping him to his knees. He was the priority—he'd lost more blood than Jax, and that much hawthorn crammed into his body posed a major risk of permanent damage. If I could get the stakes out quickly, his natural healing would hopefully kick in. Then we could use his vampire blood to heal Jax.

Forcing a smile, I said, "No offense, Elian, but this is

the *worst* rescue attempt ever. It's like you've never even seen a superhero movie."

"Sparrow." He cupped my face with a bloody hand, too weak to even smile back.

I hadn't seen him since that night in the bedroom with Jax when he'd refused to kiss me, and suddenly there he was, his blood on my face, regret heavy in his voice, the scent of death sharp on the air...

All of it threatened to break me.

"I'll fix this," I said firmly, trying to convince us both. "Hold still."

A brutal cough rattled through his chest, wet and wheezing. When he looked at me again, his eyes were glassy, his brow wrinkled in pain and confusion. He blinked slowly, then looked up at our captors.

"Evander," he whispered, but then shook his head, his brow knitting in confusion as if he no longer recognized the name.

I had no idea who Evander was, or why Elian was so oddly fixated on Keradoc, but it would have to wait.

"Elian," I said, "listen to me. We need to remove these stakes, and—"

"No," he panted, shifting his attention back to me. A new urgency flashed through his eyes, clearing away the haze. "You must... get out. Run, sparrow. You... go."

All around us the magick flickered, the guards hitting the wall with fae magick and weapons both,

Keradoc pacing like an animal trying to sniff out the weak spot.

"Haley." Jax coughed, blood splattering his lips. "It was Gem. She... she betrayed... You need to leave."

"Gem?" I gasped. "Shit. Shit! Okay. Guys? I need you both to stay focused. Jax, we can heal you with Elian's blood. He just needs a minute to regain his strength. I need to get these stakes out, so shut up and let me concentrate."

Elian pushed my hands away, dark blood leaking from his mouth in a seemingly endless stream. "Go. Find... find Hudson and—" Another wet cough strangled his words.

Next to us, Jax sucked in a sharp breath and closed his eye, a shiver rattling his body.

He could sense it, I realized. My fear.

It surged up inside me, but quickly fizzled in the wake of another emotion.

Raw, unchecked rage.

Fuck. This.

I *refused* to be scared. There was no reason for it. Both of them were going to be just fine. Hudson was fine. All of us were absolutely fucking *fine*. We just needed to get on our feet—first mission. That was our lasagna. Stop the fucking bleeding and get these guys back on their feet.

"Here's the deal, Elian," I snapped. "I'm really mad at you, asshole. Like, *really* mad. For a lot of things, not the least of which—" I gripped his shoulder and unceremoniously yanked out one of the stakes. "—is your vanishing act this week. We don't hear from you for days, and suddenly you show up shot full of hawthorn and dragged in by armed guards like a stuck pig?" I ripped out another stake, enjoying his grunts of agony. "What kind of vampire *does* that? God, I should put you out of your misery right now. One less cocky, obstinate, irredeemable bloodsucking fuckstick in the world." Another stake removed, another clattering to the ground as Keradoc and his guards continued their assault on my barrier. "But you know what, Elian? *That* would be giving you an easy out, and you haven't earned it. So if you fucking die on me here? Yeah. We're gonna have a *serious* problem—way more serious than a few branches of hawthorn impaling your chest." I freed the last stake, then met his eyes once more. Not taking any chances, I sliced open my wrist with the stake, sucked the wound to get the blood flowing, then jammed it against his mouth. "Now feed, before I shove every last one of these stakes back in and finish the job Keradoc's guards started."

He tried to turn away, but the temptation of my fresh blood on his lips was too much to resist, as I knew it would be. He grabbed my wrist with a trembling hand and licked the wound, then sucked, his eyes locked on mine in a fierce battle of wills. We both knew he had no choice but to feed, but he wasn't about to do it happily.

Too bad. I needed him alive more than I needed him happy.

Ignoring the surge of pleasure in my veins, I let him take his fill, waiting until the first pangs of dizziness hit me before I finally tore my wrist from his mouth.

The color had returned to his face, the haze clearing from his eyes. The gaping wounds in his chest started closing. Slowly, but still. Progress.

Blood ran down my arm. I lowered it to my side and curled my fingers, letting it pool in the cup of my hand until it coated my ring. Then, pressing my hand to the floor, I whispered another spell. The magickal shield brightened in response, but the incessant barrage of dark fae magick was taking its toll.

We didn't have much time.

"We need to help Jax," I said to Elian.

Wiping the blood from his mouth, he nodded and crawled over to the demon, who was turning paler by the second. Elian bit into his wrist and held it to Jax's mouth, urging him to drink as I carefully removed the bolts.

Even with the healing magick of vampire blood coursing through his system, Jax's wounds would still take time to heal. But devil's traps could drain a demon's life force at the soul level, and their removal had an immediate effect. All at once, the color returned to his skin, and after another minute, he finally turned away from Elian's vein, offering a curt nod of thanks.

"Better?" I asked.

"Nothing I won't survive." Jax wrapped an arm around

his midsection, stifling another bloody cough as he scrambled to his feet.

I helped Elian up, and the three of us let out a collective sigh.

"Gem betrayed us," Elian said, leaning on me hard. A slight tremor still rattled his muscles, reverberating into my shoulder. "We planned for everything—*everything* but that."

Anger rolled off him in hot waves, infecting me and Jax both.

"We'll deal with her later," Jax said. "We need to find a way out."

"There are too many of them." I blew out a breath. "Once this barrier drops, they'll attack us."

"If Keradoc wanted us dead," Jax said, "we'd already be in the moat."

"Agreed," I said, "but there's a lot of gray area between keeping someone alive and keeping them alive and *unharmed.* I'm really not in the mood to get my ass kicked."

"You might not have a choice tonight, angel." He nodded at the show of force. The guards who weren't working on dismantling the barrier had their weapons drawn, every last one of them waiting for their shot—waiting for Keradoc to order them to take it.

Keradoc glared at me through the barrier, his eyes blazing, his rage so palpable I could practically taste it.

Even through the magick, his sweet rose scent stung the back of my nose.

Memories collided suddenly in my mind, making me shiver. The dance, the sound of my name on his lips, the ferocity of our kiss, all of it spinning around my head like he'd spun me around that ballroom...

My magick flickered.

"Sparrow." Elian leaned close, his body still trembling and weak. "You... you need to go."

On my other side, Jax nodded. "We'll hold them off. You break for it."

"Shut up," I snapped. "Both of you. We go out together, or we go down together. Non-negotiable."

They tried to argue, but it was pointless. I'd no sooner leave them behind than they'd leave me. The problem was neither of them was strong enough to walk out of here without a lot of help—not when we'd still have to fight our way past the guards and whatever else awaited us outside this room, not to mention the party still raging down on the main level.

Shit, shit, shit!

Where was Hudson? What the hell had Gem done? Where had she gone? Was she still in the castle, waiting in the shadows for another opportunity to stab us in the back?

I glanced around frantically for another escape, my

magick waning. Everywhere I looked, I saw another guard. Another obstacle. Another dead end.

I wanted to roar. After all that blood and magick, after finally getting the guys on their feet, we were no better off than when Keradoc's guards had dumped them on the floor. Elian didn't have the strength for a vampire blur, Jax didn't have the energy to work his fear mojo, and my magick was completely tapped out.

The barrier surrounding us faded to a dull pink.

We had minutes. Maybe seconds.

The guys closed ranks around me.

And then, with nothing more than a soft hiss, the magick fizzled out, leaving us completely exposed.

4

HALEY

"Hold your fire." Keradoc lifted a hand to the guards behind us, but his eyes were locked on mine, his gaze triumphant.

I felt Jax and Elian tense beside me, both of them spring-loaded for an attack.

"Don't," I whispered. "We're severely outnumbered."

"Never stopped us before," Jax said.

"Certain death?" Elian laughed. "I like the odds here, brother."

"Guys," I warned, but it was too late.

For two supernaturals who acted like they wanted to murder each other on the best of days, they sure didn't have any trouble teaming up to ignore me.

As one, they sprang into action and lunged for Keradoc, and I watched with fresh horror as two bolts zinged through the air, nailing them both in the back.

Once again, my men fell to their knees.

Unruffled, Keradoc stepped swiftly past them, brushing off his shoulder. He was still dressed in his party finery—black silks and leather swirled with delicate silver and violet embellishments—and if not for the sheen of sweat on his brow and the tiny flecks of blood dotting his cheek, he would've looked like the perfect gentleman and host.

He still hadn't dropped his gaze from mine, and as he approached, I felt powerless to do anything but watch... and wait.

Gone was the faltering glamour I'd seen earlier, leaving only Keradoc in its place—sharp jaw, penetrating violet eyes, sensual mouth.

Everything about him appeared kingly and entitled, his movements slow and deliberate, and in that moment, I wanted nothing more than to see the fae's dark head on a pike.

Yet the longer he stared at me, the farther my thoughts strayed, sweeping me up again in the memory of that sensual mouth claiming mine, his hands in my hair, his cock grinding against me on the dais...

I closed my eyes and took a step back, trying to shake myself loose from the grip of those images. From the feelings they unleashed inside me, hot and prickly and terrifying.

Intriguing.

When I opened my eyes again, the bastard was still watching me, a new glimmer shining in his violet eyes.

He arched a delicate eyebrow, as if he'd been reading my thoughts.

Through the burn of my cheeks, I lifted my chin, refusing to be cowed.

The situation was grim, sure, but not impossible. Like Jax had said—if Keradoc wanted us dead, we'd be swimming with the ghouls by now. He'd already admitted he needed me for the ancestor spell, which meant I had some leverage to play with. And since the guys were still in possession of their heads, even after attempting another attack against him, maybe they had some leverage too.

It was a thin hope based on even thinner logic, but with Jax and Elian immobilized, Hudson MIA, and no other friends in sight, that hope was all I had to cling to.

He finally stopped before me, so close I could see all the shades of color in his irises. Not just violet, I realized now, but violet flecked with gold, ringed in deep indigo, the colors seeming to shift before me in an endless dance. He lowered his gaze to my mouth, and I sucked in a sharp breath, heat snaking down my spine.

Kiss me like that again, Daughter of Darkwinter, and I'll be whoever you need me to be...

"A heroic attempt, Miss Barnes," Keradoc said, and it took me a beat to realize he was talking about the blood magick, not my kiss. "Truly. But as I'm sure your companions can attest to—assuming their brief sojourn to the earthly realm didn't wipe the lesson from memory—Midnight has no need of heroes." Still glaring at me, he snapped his fingers, and several of the guards stepped forward. "Put the two fugitives in a cell. I'll deal with them later."

Jax and Elian groaned in protest, but groaning was about all they had the strength for. The guards grabbed them roughly. Elian coughed up more blood.

"If you still expect me to do your bidding, warlord," I said firmly, choking back my panic, "I expect you to leave my men unharmed."

"Your so-called men are nothing but lowly fugitives. They gave up the right to fair treatment the night they plotted with the dark goddess to betray me, defy their sentences, and escape my realm."

I narrowed my eyes. The dark goddess? *Melantha* had helped them escape?

No wonder she knew about them—knew to send me to New Orleans to ask for Elian's help.

My mind reeled with new questions, but there was no time to ask them. The guards were already hauling Elian and Jax out, leaving a trail of blood in their wake.

"Give the order," I said, "or all of this will have been for nothing. I don't care what you and Melantha hold over my head. I won't help you if you hurt them, Keradoc. That's a promise."

The muscle in Keradoc's jaw ticked in annoyance, but after making me suffer through another long, admonishing glare, he finally nodded.

"Remove the bolts and dress their wounds," he told the guards. "Keep the demon and the fae together, isolated from the other prisoners."

"And give them food and water," I added. "*Fresh* food and *clean* water."

Another glare. Another sigh. And finally, a half-nod. "Water," he said. "For now."

It was more than I expected, so I kept my mouth shut.

"And the witch?" one of the guards asked.

"Leave her." Keradoc's teeth flashed in the torchlight, and he leaned closer once more, reaching for a lock of my hair. In a soft, soothing voice that sent chills racing across my shoulders, he whispered, "It's time I had a conversation with my little thief about consequences."

5

HALEY

I was alone again with the warlord of Midnight, my insides trembling as he continued to stare at me, cold and unflinching. It felt like he was looking right through me, peeling back every layer, dismantling every wall I'd spent so many years erecting.

I studied him as well, still trying to understand what I'd seen behind his glamour. He was the warlord of Midnight—at least, that was the role he was playing. So why did he need to hide behind a mask?

More disturbing than that, though, was the strange connection I felt to him. Not just because of the intense kiss we'd shared, or because I'd used my magick to influence the flow of his blood, or even because I'd *sworn* I'd seen Elian's silver eyes flickering behind Keradoc's violet ones.

No... Something *else* bound me to this fae—a dark

magick that hummed between us like an electrical current, barely perceptible but lingering nevertheless. My body responded to his presence even now, drawn to him in ways a captive should never be.

And in those violet eyes, I saw it too—the same curiosity about me as I felt about him. The same wonder.

The same desire.

After what seemed like an eternity, he finally turned his back and headed for the exit.

The breath rushed from my lungs in an audible sigh.

"Come," he demanded, the sharp, icy tone echoing with his footsteps across the floor.

I was still vibrating from the adrenaline coursing through my system, weakened from the magick I'd conjured, terrified for Jax and Elian, completely confused about my reactions to the man, and also—for the record—starving. Unless he was promising me dinner, I had no intentions of following that asshole *anywhere* alone.

When he realized I hadn't moved, he stopped before the exit, barely turning his head to spare me a glance. "Is there a problem, Miss Barnes?"

"I was waiting for you to say 'please,' but apparently, you're about as big a fan of manners as you are of free choice, so it looks like I'm pretty much screwed."

"Categorically untrue." He approached me again, his eyes glinting with some new trickery. "I'm a huge proponent of choice. In this moment, you've got two: follow me out of this room on your own two feet, or I shall render you unconscious and drag you out by the hair. Take your pick, witch, and make haste. I've got business to attend to."

"Wow. So the big, scary fairy gets off on making idle threats to women. *Very* impressive, Keradoc. You totally deserve a cookie." I rolled my eyes and stalked past him, knocking into his shoulder.

In a move so fluid it was no more than a blur in my peripheral vision, he spun and gripped my upper arms, hauling me backward against his chest. His fingers dug so hard into my flesh I knew he'd leave a bruise.

In a low, dangerous voice, he whispered, "Would you prefer I show rather than tell? Even in a realm so brutal as ours, I'm *not* known for my mercy."

"Really? And here I thought you were a big ol' softy, what with you beheading a pair of shifters, sending your guards to ambush my men with crossbows, tossing them into the dungeon half-dead and bleeding, not to mention drugging me with your fae roofies." I jerked free of his grip and turned to face him, rubbing my throbbing arms. "Twice, I might add. And I don't care how many guards you have at your beck and call. You manhandle me like that again, the next time I work my magick, I'll blast it straight up your arrogant fae ass."

A slow grin stretched across his mouth, a menacing slash of red in a face too pretty to be so dark. "You think me cruel, little thief?"

"Among other things, yes."

"Cruelty is a tactic that wins wars."

"Cruelty is a tactic relied upon by men with small dicks who lack the confidence to communicate and the courage to fight fair."

"I see. So in your neat-and-tidy little worldview, the meek shall inherit the earth—or in this case, Midnight?" He scoffed. "Only two kinds of people believe that, Miss Barnes. The extremely privileged and the extremely naive, neither of whom have any right to criticize the things the rest of us must do to survive."

Survive. The word pricked at my insides, igniting a flurry of fresh outrage.

"You aren't a survivor, Keradoc," I practically spat. "You're the reason people like me are forced to survive. You stand there reeking of wealth and power, smiling for your guests, opening your home to the masses as if you're some benevolent god from above when in reality you're nothing but a murderer, a kidnapper, a torturer, and a warmonger with legions of minions falling over themselves for a chance to do your bidding. The only battles your sword has ever seen are the ones dropped at your feet for your entertainment, and you know *nothing* about my life—nothing but the few things you believe will serve your interests. So the next time you want to lecture me about privilege and naiveté, you pompous dick, do your fucking homework."

This time, I didn't turn away or try to stalk past him. I stared him down, fury simmering between us, waiting for him to make another move—to tie me up again, to blow his gold fairy dust into my face, to gut me with the dagger he'd stolen from me.

But Keradoc only glared at me, the indignation in his eyes warring with his unchecked curiosity and, if I didn't know any better, arousal.

Saying nothing, he finally turned and marched toward the door. This time, he didn't stop to see if I was following, and for the briefest instant, I considered bolting in the other direction, taking my chances with another doorway, a window, anything but whatever Keradoc had in store for me.

But Gem had already betrayed us. The guys had been ambushed. Keradoc knew the game right from the start, and he'd likely planned for every contingency.

If there was truly another escape, he wouldn't have turned his back on me.

I closed my eyes. Drew a deep breath.

Survive, I told myself, the word never far from my thoughts. *No matter what.*

It was my next piece of lasagna—make it through the night alive. Not just for myself, but for Jax and Elian. For Hudson, wherever he was. For my sisters. I had no idea if Melantha knew I'd failed in my quest to retrieve Keradoc's blood, but right now, I had to hope she didn't. Had to hope that my sisters were okay.

And as much as it burned me to admit it, that fae asshole was my best shot at coming up with a plan to keep them safe. Melantha was as much Keradoc's enemy as she was mine. That right there was some common ground.

Something I could potentially exploit as readily as he was planning to exploit my Darkwinter connection.

Survive. The word echoed once more.

I nodded. Shored up my walls. Promised myself I'd do just that.

And right now, surviving meant putting one foot in front of the other and following my captor into the dark abyss that awaited me.

6

HALEY

With smooth, graceful steps, Keradoc led me down the long corridor outside the throne room and up a narrow, winding staircase that climbed so high, I grew dizzier with every step. There was no railing and no light to guide the way, only the glint of silver on his clothing a few steps ahead and the cold, damp stone surrounding us—sometimes smooth and polished, other times as rough and unrefined as the walls of a cave.

Again I thought about slicing my palm, trying to tap back into my magick. But I was running on empty, in desperate need of food and sleep, and worried about the guys. Fear and exhaustion? Perfect formula for sloppy mistakes. Keradoc would be expecting another attack, and we'd already encountered a dozen more guards, some pacing the halls, others scuttling down the stairs like roaches, their armor and weapons brushing my chest as I stepped aside to let them pass.

Best I just bide my time. Gather my strength. Observe, assess, and make a plan.

My thighs and calves burned with every step, but finally, after what felt like hours, we reached the top of the staircase. It was all I could do not to drop to my hands and knees and kiss the ground.

The landing opened up right in the center of a massive gallery that stretched out about fifty feet in both directions, with towering stained-glass windows at each end like some kind of gothic cathedral. The walls were the same rough-hewn black stone as the staircase, only now they glowed a soft orange from dozens of magickal chandeliers hanging from the ceiling, the endless black rock broken only by a series of ornately carved oak doors. I had no idea what lay beyond them, but the whole place was, like so much of Midnight, strangely beautiful and intriguing.

"The entire castle was once a mountain," Keradoc said, his voice softening with a hint of wonder that took me by surprise. "Legend has it the trolls carved it into a castle with their bare hands."

"Trolls? They're a thing here?"

"No one knows for certain. None have been sighted for a good five hundred years or so." This time, the smile he shared was playful rather than cruel, and damn if it didn't send a little spark to my heart. "Fear not, Miss Barnes. Should any trolls breach the walls and attempt to reclaim their home, I shall personally slaughter them and present their heads to you on silver platters."

I shrugged as if his teasing *hadn't* thrown me completely off guard. "If you're looking for the perfect gift, K-Doc, I'm more of a chocolates-and-weapons kinda girl. Actually, if you wouldn't mind returning that dagger you stole from me and sending me on my merry little way, we'll call it even. Hell, I'll even send you a thank-you card when I get back home."

He shook his head, his eyes dancing in the light. He looked younger somehow, as if a little teasing had the power to erase years of brutal existence.

Maybe it did.

"Fair offer," he said with a wink, "but I think I'll pass, clever little thief."

"Worth a shot, though, right?"

"I suppose so." Still smiling, he gestured for me to follow him once more, and together we continued down the left branch to the very end of the hallway. He paused before a set of carved double doors, each side boasting one half of a massive tree lush with star-shaped leaves.

The craftsmanship was exquisite—a delicate, beautiful work of art that seemed out of place in this hall of rough stone.

"Wow," I breathed, unable to stop myself from reaching

out. At the slightest brush of my fingertips against the polished wood, the leaves glimmered with silver light. "That's incredible!"

"The doors were crafted by the fae, of course. Trolls aren't known for their artistry." Keradoc grabbed the polished door handles, then turned to me once more, his face so close I could see the silver light of the leaves reflected in his dark pupils. "The entire floor comprises the living quarters for myself and my guests—primarily fae nobles and their families, or the occasional military commander. More often than not, it's just me and my…" He trailed off, the barest breath of sadness lingering.

You and your what? I wanted to ask. *Partner? Concubines? Imaginary friends?*

I closed my eyes and blew out a breath, trying to shore up my walls again. Every minute passed in Keradoc's presence only confused me further, shaking my confidence and sending my nerves into hyperdrive. Who *was* this man? This enigmatic fae? In the span of a couple of hours, he'd gone from legendary warlord to smooth-as-silk conversationalist to ballroom charmer to illusionist to kidnapper, and now he was showing me around the castle like a proud homeowner welcoming an old friend?

"As much as I appreciate the historic-homes-of-Midnight tour," I said, opening my eyes to meet his intense gaze again, "why did you bring me up here, Keradoc?

Where are my men? Is this all just... just a game of show-and-tell to you? What am I *doing* here?"

My questions erased the last of the mirth between us, and his gaze turned as cold as the walls, his jaw tightening, his spine straightening as if he just remembered he was supposed to be detached and demanding, not friendly or playful. With a great sigh, he pushed open the massive doors and stepped aside, gesturing for me to enter ahead of him.

Another command.

I did as he asked, immediately drawn in by the sight before me. It was a massive suite, featuring a large common room with a fireplace, several couches, and an eating area set along the back with a dining table fit for a dozen people. A row of tall, glass-front doors opened onto a balcony offering a stunning view of the city and the mountains to the east—the Dead Claw range, if I remembered right. There were two large bathrooms accessible from inside the suite as well as from the main hall, both with massive black onyx tubs I was already dying to sink into. At equal intervals around the common room, I counted six alcoves carved right into the stone, each one large enough for a four-poster bed, an armoire, and a small desk. More magickal chandeliers hung from the ceiling in every room, flickering in time with the fire.

Like everything else in the castle, the suite was a mix of medieval royal opulence and primitive, rough-hewn architecture that made me feel like we'd tunneled into some ancient dwarven city beneath the mountains.

"Stunning," I whispered, though I hadn't meant to say it out loud.

"I'm pleased you think so," Keradoc said from behind me, his sudden nearness startling. I'd been so lost in the splendor of it all, I hadn't sensed his approach. "This is your home now, Miss Barnes. Take your pick of the bedrooms and make yourself comfortable. I'll have some clothing sent up for you later."

Though I sensed it was coming, his words hit the bottom of my stomach like cold rocks. It didn't matter how beautiful his castle was or what comforts he was promising. All the opulence in the world couldn't disguise what this place truly was.

"This is no home," I hissed, whirling around to face him. "It's a prison."

"You're not my prisoner."

"No?" I pressed a hand to my chest, feigning a relieved laugh. "Wow, so glad we cleared *that* up. Awkward! Anyway, if you'll kindly show me to the dungeons to collect my friends, we'll be on our way. Great party, though. We'll have to do it again a year from never."

"I cannot allow you to leave the castle unguarded. But that's merely a safety precaution. And just for tonight, I'd like you to remain in your suite—there are too many unsavory guests afoot, most of whom have the manners of wild boars. But once I'm rid of them, you'll be free to wander the castle as you wish. I'll show you the kitchens tomorrow, the gardens... well, what passes for gardens in Midnight. You'll have free reign."

"Gardens?" I mocked. "Why didn't you say so? You're right—totally not a prison. Do I have to sign up for my time in the yard? When do I meet my cellmate? I sure hope we have the same taste in music!"

"Throw a tantrum if you must, but I think you'll find me quite accommodating, provided you hold up your end of the bargain."

"We're bargaining now, are we? I don't recall any negotiations. You're getting your weapon. What am I getting?"

"You and your companions are still breathing, are you not? That will continue to be the case for as long as you continue to cooperate."

"Yeah? And how long do you expect me to stay here, *cooperating*?" I made air quotes around the word.

"As long as it takes you to craft the ritual, call upon your Darkwinter ancestors, and secure our victory."

A bitter laugh slipped from my lips. "Let's get something straight, Keradoc. War is *your* game. *Your* victory. I'm just a pawn, so stop pretending there's anything mutual about it."

He opened his mouth to respond, but a sharp rap on the door cut him off.

"Enter," he said gruffly.

A fae woman with hair the color of pale sapphires and eyes the same shade of violet as Keradoc's stepped through the doorway, escorted by two fae guards. All three wore the same dark-gray military uniform, but significantly more patches and pins decorated hers.

The guy on her right was a new face, but I recognized the one on her left as the fucker who'd kicked Elian in the back in the throne room. He glared at me now, his face contorted with unchecked hostility.

A chill skittered down my spine.

"Forgive the interruption, sir," the high-ranking fae woman said. "I come with urgent news from the north."

"What is it, Oona?" Keradoc's voice was tight and exasperated, but that's not what caught my attention.

It was the name. Oona.

Just like the fae woman Jax had loved. The one who'd supposedly died on her father's orders.

On *Keradoc's* orders.

7

HALEY

I turned away from the fae guards and stared into the fireplace, schooling my reaction.

Oona. It *had* to be the same woman. Even if Oona was a common name among the fae, what were the chances that two of them had been in Keradoc's close orbit? With violet eyes, besides?

No way. She was definitely his daughter.

So she wasn't dead, then. Which meant Elian had lied to Jax. Why?

And what would Jax do when he found out?

A mix of emotions churned through my gut—worry and sympathy for Jax, rage at Elian's capacity for treachery, and there, simmering beneath it all, a big helping of red-hot jealousy.

I shoved it all aside though, forcing myself to take in whatever information I could.

"Two warships bearing the standard of Darkwinter have been spotted near the harbor," she reported. "None have disembarked—presumably on account of the Fog—but it's only a matter of time. The Fog is already beginning to thin."

Fog? Was she serious?

"Your enemies are afraid of a little fog," I blurted out, turning to face Keradoc, "and you think you need *my* help?"

"The Fog of a Thousand Knives, Miss Barnes," he said. "So named for its ability to slice anyone it touches into ribbons so microscopic, whole bodies become liquified in seconds."

Bile rose in my throat at the thought.

Keradoc must've seen the revulsion and fear on my face. His eyes softened, and he joined me by the fireplace, his voice low and soothing when he said, "Amaranth City is the safest place in the realm, and the castle is the safest place in the city. Neither the fog nor the enemy will reach us here."

He touched my shoulder, his skin warm, his eyes gentle. For a moment, it felt like we were the only people in the room.

I wanted that momentary comfort... and I hated him for it.

For all of it—the cruelty, the imprisonment, the beheadings, the way he'd allowed his guards to treat Jax and Elian. But mostly, I hated the kindness in his eyes, the softness in his touch. It was all a lie, another fae manipulation designed to weaken my defenses.

"And which enemy are you referring to this time?" I asked. "From what I hear, you've got a whole list of monsters waiting in line for a chance to chop off your head and mount it on the wall like a trophy."

All the kindness in his eyes drained away, leaving only the ice-cold warlord behind.

Good. I'd much rather face the ugly truth than a beautiful lie.

"Children playing war games do not concern me, Daughter of Darkwinter," he said, his voice loud enough for everyone to hear now. "Your esteemed ancestors, however, *do* concern me."

Turning back to Oona, he said, "What else?"

"Dead Claw, sir. There's another Darkwinter party on the eastern front moving north toward Stone City."

The muscle in Keradoc's jaw ticked. "Alert the squadron at the Stone City outpost they've got Darkwinter inbound, if they're not already aware. I want those bastards stopped before they get anywhere near the wall."

"Consider it done, sir."

With a curt nod, he dismissed them, then joined me once more at the fireplace.

None of this made sense. If she was Keradoc's daughter, why did she speak to him so formally? Was that just a military thing? And if he and his guards had ever truly threatened her relationship with Jax, why did she seem to respect the man so much? The way she looked at him went beyond a daughter's love for a father or even a general's respect for her commanding officer. It bordered on admiration.

I had a million questions but for now, I held my tongue, waiting for Keradoc to make the next move.

"Do we understand each other yet, Daughter of Darkwinter? Or do you need additional persuading? I would be more than happy to have your friends moved to... less hospitable accommodations than they're currently enjoying, and that's saying something."

Thoughts of Jax and Elian shivering their assess off in some rank dungeon zapped the last of my strength. The craziness of the evening caught up with me in a rush, tears stinging my eyes, my limbs trembling with exhaustion. Suddenly, all I wanted to do was curl into a ball and pass out in front of the fire.

"I'll do as you ask, Keradoc," I said wearily. "Because you're holding us hostage and I've got no good choices here. But I'm telling you—I don't know the spell to summon my ancestors, I've got literally *zero* connection to them, and I can't perform a summoning ritual of that magnitude and complexity under pressure. Even if I was on board with this plan—which, make a note of this for posterity, I'm absolutely *not*—it's not something we can force."

"Force? No. But plan and prepare for? Together? That's something we can certainly do." He stepped close again, his sweet scent drenching the air around me. "I'm not the enemy, Miss Barnes. Remember that."

His smile was sad, his eyes softening as he captured me in another entrancing gaze, and like a fool I let my mind fall back into memories of that kiss.

"Haley," he whispered, his hand reaching for mine, our fingers brushing.

"You know nothing of it," I hissed. But of course it was bullshit.

My gaze dropped to his mouth, my stomach fizzy as he leaned in close, his warm breath tickling my lips as he...

Clamped a cold iron cuff over my wrist.

"What... what is this?" Shaking free of the trance, I clawed at the iron uselessly. "What have you done?"

Magick bit into my skin. Dark magick. *His* magick, crawling up one arm and down the other, spreading through my veins like ice. My teeth began to chatter, my skin erupting in goosebumps.

"Relax, Darkwinter," he said, shaking out his fingers. They looked red, as if they'd just been burned.

The cuff, I realized. Iron was poisonous to fae.

"It won't harm you," he said. "It's merely a dampener cuff. It will ensure your magick can't be used in an attack or in any other way that might undermine or harm me during your stay."

I cursed myself for being so stupid. So weak. Why had I let my guard down around him? Why had I thought, even for a second, that he was capable of even a shred of compassion?

"And you expect me to perform a complicated blood ritual while neutered?" I snapped, still trying to pry off the cuff. "I'm not sure you've thought this all the way through, genius."

"You're not neutered, just muted. You'll still be able to practice summoning spells and other small magicks, provided they're not intended for use against me or my guards or staff. Then, when the time is right to call upon your ancestors, the cuff will be removed and you'll have access to your full power."

"Yeah? And what makes you so sure I'll behave myself on *that* night if you don't trust me to do it now?"

"I have every confidence you and I will have reached an understanding by then. Perhaps even a level of trust."

"Right now, I trust you to be a complete asshole, and I don't see that changing any time soon."

"Nevertheless, this is your reality now. I suggest you make peace with it, and channel all that fire into crafting an effective ritual. Now, I must return to the party and ensure the remaining guests are ushered away without incident. If there's anything I can do to make your stay more palatable, well…" The grin returned, only now it was the grin of a dark wolf, his eyes shimmering like raw amethyst in the firelight. "My chambers are right down the hall. Should any *needs* arise…" His eyes trailed down my body, then back up, blazing a hot path. "Don't hesitate to knock on my door."

"I'd rather knock your head into the wall."

"You could certainly try." He gave me a small, mocking bow. "I remain, as ever, at your service."

And with that, Keradoc of Midnight was gone, leaving me furious, bone-tired, and—worst of all—dangerously, impossibly, *ridiculously* aroused.

"Fae magick," I said, desperate to convince myself that's all it was. "Hell of a drug."

8

ELIAN

"Are we dead yet, brother? Wasn't expecting the afterlife to smell so rank."

Yeah. Jax hadn't said a word, and I was talking to the fucking shadows again. Shadows and rats and the ghosts of ten thousand men who'd taken their last broken breaths in this dungeon long before we showed up.

How long had it even been since they'd staked us, beaten us, thrown us down here?

Hours? Days? An eternity?

There was only one way into the dungeon—the steel door they'd dragged us through—and no one had come or gone since.

The whole place reeked of death.

Jax and I were shoved into one of a handful of barred cells, all of them empty but for a lone prisoner in the cell directly across from ours. Now, a pained gasp emanated from his side of the dungeon, but I had no idea who or what lurked behind those bars. It was so dark, I couldn't make out much of anything beyond our immediate area—beyond the wet stone and waste and the moldy rags that were probably once prisoners, their bones picked clean by rats. It hurt to breathe. Hell, I wasn't even sure I remembered how. Everything attached to me was bleeding and raw, inside and out, and my whole body trembled with a gaping, soul-sucking need for *one* thing. One fucking little black pill to make it all go away.

But that old Devil wasn't dancing with me tonight. Only those ever-shifting shadows and my rancid thoughts and the demon I still called my brother, slumped against the damp stone wall right next to me, the sound of his ragged heartbeat and the acrid scent of his warm, hellspawn blood the only evidence he was still here with me.

Hell, maybe he *wasn't* here. Maybe we'd died in that throne room together on our knees, and this was our purgatory. Or maybe we'd never even escaped Midnight at all. Maybe the last two years in New Orleans had all been a fucking dream and we'd been trapped in the dungeons the whole time, wasting away breath by breath. Memory by memory.

"Jax," I whispered for what felt like the hundredth time. "Jax."

No response but the squeaking of another rodent

gnawing at what I now realized was a festering corpse in the far corner. A red-haired fae from another realm, naked and long since forgotten.

My mind spun, still trying to piece together how everything had gone to shit at the Feast of the Beast.

The pain of Gem's betrayal cut through me anew. How could she have set us up like that? How had I not seen it coming?

And Keradoc... What game of illusions was he playing? For those few hazy moments, kneeling in a pool of my own blood before the dais, I'd looked upon his face and seen...

No. Impossible. Just more ghosts and wishful thinking and the byproducts of a mind long ago poisoned by drugs and fantasies.

"But I could've *sworn* it was him," I said anyway, as if I still needed someone to convince me otherwise. "Silver eyes. Those silver fucking eyes. I saw them, Jax. Clear as the first moon. But then they vanished. *He* vanished. Fucking illusion magick, or... I don't know. Another one of Melantha's games or the Dream finally scrambling up whatever's left of my brain."

Next to me, Jax coughed, the sound of it rattling through his chest. I'd taken out the second round of bolts and fed him more of my blood, but healing was slow going for both of us. The guards weren't exactly gentle when they tossed us into the cell, and the water Keradoc was supposed to send us still hadn't materialized.

"I lost him again," I said, my mind swirling in and out of consciousness, traveling through time and memory. "All of them. They were never the same after that. It should've been me, Jax. Not him. He was the good one. It should've been me."

Jax coughed again, the scent of a fresh spray of blood tingeing the air.

My stomach churned with hunger for it, but even if I'd wanted to drain him dry, the demon blood wouldn't sustain me, and there were no humans down here. Not tonight.

"Did you ever have one?" I asked, my speech starting to slur. "A family? Were you someone's son? A father? A brother?"

At that, the demon finally spoke, every word gritted out through teeth clenched in pain. "What the *fuck* are you on about, Saint? A brother? More blood and roses bullshit?"

"My family... my fae family. A long time ago."

"You had a family? Good for you. They know what a fuckup you are?"

"Yeah, I think they might."

"And Haley? What about her. What about *her*, you fuck? You left us days ago without a word, nothing more than some bullshit note, and I defended you. I looked into her sad, worried face and actually defended you. Where the fuck were you?"

"With Gem. Figuring out the plan, just like I said."

"Trading secrets with the enemy. Playing right into her fucking trap."

"If I'd known she was planning to stab us in the back, I would've—"

Jax coughed again, cutting me off.

Just as well. When it came down to it, I had no explanation. No excuses. I was the one who'd trusted her, who'd spent so much time with her—then and now. I should've seen it coming. Yeah, Gem was an old friend—one who'd proven her loyalty long ago. But still. There *had* to have been signs. Signs I fucking missed, and *that* was on me.

"I'd say I was sorry," I said, "but I don't think you're the one who needs to hear it."

"You sure about that, asshole?"

"Haley—"

"*Don't*," Jax warned. With a surge of renewed energy, he shot out a hand and clamped it around my throat. "Say her name again, bloodsucker, and I'll tear off your fucking head."

"I damn near destroyed her, Jax," I rasped. "Again. So many fucking times, and she didn't deserve it. *Doesn't* deserve it. All my bullshit and the secrets and the lies and... *Fuck*." I was rambling again, memories and regrets crashing through my mind faster than I could parse them. Beneath the demon's crushing grip, fresh fear tightened my throat, churning through me like gasoline waiting for the match. "She was taken. She was taken because she trusted me—once again—to take care of her. And once again, I failed. I failed the woman I was supposed to love and protect and fucking cherish for the rest of my pathetic immortal life. And where did that immortality get me? I'm shot full of holes that won't heal right because my blood is tainted, and I'm locked up in this shithole, trapped in this dank-ass prison in the worst place in the fucking universe with no company but a dying demon who'd just as soon see my ashes in an urn, and all I've got to show for it is—"

"Saint, you're on my *last* fucking nerve right now and believe me, after what we just went through? I don't have any nerves left to spare." Jax jerked his hand away, and I sucked in a breath. "So either make a *fucking* point, or shut up and let me think, because one of us has to figure out how to get out of this mess—to find Hudson and get Haley back and get her *far* the fuck away from Keradoc—and clearly you're not the man for the job. In fact, you're not the man for *any* job, because you can't even go five minutes without killing someone or blowing something up or creating a major catastrophe the rest of us have to clean up and you know what, asshole? Yeah, I *would* like to see your ashes in an urn. Because I'm exhausted. You fucking *exhaust* me, *Saint* Elian. So right now, I need you to do me and Hudson and the woman you claim to love and the dead guy rotting behind us and every last bog roach in this dungeon a favor and stop. Fucking. Talking."

Stop fucking talking? Stop fucking talking.

Yeah, I could do that. I could definitely do that. I *wanted* to do that—one right thing in a lifetime of utter wrongs, but suddenly the walls were closing in and the air was evaporating and my heart wanted to pound right out of my chest and I couldn't fucking breathe...

"Jax," I gasped. "Wait. I'm not... I'm not well. It's the... the... the..." I lifted a hand, the tremor so severe it was all just a bloody blur at the edges of my vision. "I'm losing it. I'm losing... and I can't... I..."

He looked over at me then, his eye widening at the sight, a glint in the darkness. I tried to imagine what it looked like to him—me, strung out and shaking, begging, losing my shit while the rats continued to gnaw and the roaches continued to scamper and death breathed on the back of my neck...

"You're in withdrawal." He closed his eye and bit off a curse. "Perfect. Anything else you'd like to fuck up for us this evening?"

"I... I... I don't have any more pills on me. I didn't want to take anything before the Feast and I didn't bring any because I wanted a clear head and I thought we'd be back at the apartment and on our way out of this fucking realm and now I'm—"

"Now you're fucked."

I nodded, but he already knew the deal. He'd seen it enough times before.

"Did I say you were on my last nerve?" he snapped. "That was a lie. I've got none left for you, *brother*."

"But do you have... do you... the pills, Jax. Do—"

"Fuck you," he ground out, then reached into his pocket. He retrieved a small silver pillbox, tipped one of those little black beauties into his hand.

He'd always carried them, just in case. *Always*. I nearly wept.

"More," I said. I didn't even have the strength to reach for the pills myself. All I could do was beg. "More, Jax. One isn't enough. I... I need..."

He glowered at me like he really was debating ripping off my head, which... yeah. I definitely deserved it. But he shook out another pill anyway, and grabbed my jaw in a murderous grip and dropped two pills on my tongue.

I closed my mouth. Turned away from him. Moaned in relief as the drugs started to dissolve.

After a long pause, Jax sighed and said, "You need to kick this shit, Saint. If not for yourself, then for her. Do it for her."

His voice was soft—kind, even—yet it felt as if he'd just lit me on fire.

I clenched my fists in my lap, trying to keep the fury at bay. "Just because you're sharing her bed now doesn't mean you get to tell me what to do for my—"

"Your *what*, Saint?" he hissed, all the kindness evaporating. "Your long-lost love? A woman you abandoned without cause? A woman whose heart you keep on shredding every time you look at her? She's still in love with you, asshole, and all you're doing is rubbing her face in it like it's all some fucking game to you. She would've given you the world, and you turned your back on her for *this* place. How the fuck do you even live with yourself?"

If I had any strength left in me, I would've torn out his throat for that.

"You have no fucking *idea* what I did to get here," I said. "Why I did it. Why I left her and what it does to *my* fucking heart every time I look at *her*. You wanna talk about the past? You wanna compare notes? You were in Midnight long before I ever showed up, so you tell yourself whatever lies you need to about what kind of man you are, but don't you *dare* pretend you're not going to destroy her life."

He snorted out a harsh laugh, but didn't respond, and for a long while we both just sat there stewing in our own rage and misery, his heart banging around behind his busted ribs, the Dream taking its sweet time working through my bloodstream.

When Jax finally spoke again, his voice was so empty and broken I couldn't even be sure I hadn't imagined it.

"Fuck you, Elian," came the whisper, and when I forced myself to look at him, his cheeks were wet with tears. "Fuck you and everything you are and everything you did and everything we *both* fucking lost along the way."

The stale air shifted beside me, and he groaned as he pushed himself to his feet, one arm clutched around his midsection.

"Going somewhere?" I asked.

"We've got a witch to save, you dick." He kicked my thigh. "And by the way, since I'm pretty sure you and I are both going to die tonight, I might as well tell you I'm halfway in love with her. So fuck you for that, too."

The admission tore a fresh hole in my heart, but I'd known it was coming. I could see it in his eye that night he fucked her in front of me, and again when he'd come out of the room later and found me in the hallway. It wasn't just vengeance, wasn't just some twisted shit to pour salt in my wounds.

He'd already fallen under her spell. And I was pretty sure the feeling was mutual.

It killed me to even think about it, but deep down, I had to accept it. I just wanted her to be okay. To be happy, if that was even still possible. And if Jax was it for her, I'd accept it. Support it, even.

Not that I was about to admit it.

I dragged my ass to my feet, still leaning back against the wet stone for support. The Dream had settled me a bit, smoothing out some of the tremors, but it hadn't yet dropped me into the numb haze I knew was coming. It was like the calm before the storm—a brief moment of clarity and okay-ness before it sucked me in deep.

"Yeah, well, you're an asshole, Jax," I said. "You've always been an asshole. And as much as I'd love to murder you for falling in love with a woman you should've had the decency to stay far away from, I can't, because I still need your help getting her out of this hellhole and eviscerating the purple-eyed freak who took her."

"Same page, dickhead. Same page."

The words felt like a promise. An alliance, and I let them bolster me.

"The plan is still the plan," I said firmly. "Assassinate the warlord. As far as getting his blood for Haley? That's a lost cause at this point."

"Agreed."

"Once she's out of danger—"

"We're taking down Gem and the guards."

I nodded. "So you got my back on this, demon? Come what may?"

This time, he didn't hesitate.

"Blood before roses, you sick fae fuck." He smacked the back of my head, then gripped my hair, holding tight as he glared at me, and I could see from the ferocity in his eye how much he meant it this time.

How much he'd *always* meant it, despite all the shit we'd put each other through. Shit I still couldn't even bring myself to confess.

A knot of emotion tightened my throat, but I swallowed it down. Buried it.

"Whatever happens tonight, brother," I said, "we're getting her out."

"We're getting us *all* out."

I shook my head, adamant. "Haley comes first. That was *always* the deal, and nothing's changed on that front."

He let out a heavy sigh, but then he nodded, and once again I trusted it. Whether he wanted to admit it or not, the demon was *more* than halfway in love with her. He'd do whatever was in his power to keep her safe, just like Hudson would.

"Any ideas where our gargoyle might be?" I asked, fresh worry chewing through my gut. Hudson was fierce and I knew he could look out for himself, but it wasn't like him to no-show when we were in deep shit. Something was definitely wrong.

"He's not here," Jax said. "If he was, he would've been the first one storming that throne room the second trouble hit."

"Let's hope he's in a better place than we are."

"Hope isn't a viable strategy, Saint. Chances are, we're looking at another rescue mission. That's if he's still—"

"He is. And we'll find him." I blew out a shaky breath, knowing our chances were slim to none on all fronts, but we had to fucking try. "Once we figure out how to bust out of here, I want you to head up—"

A new commotion from outside the main door cut me off—sounded like the guards returning. Arguing.

Suddenly, the door heaved open, bathing the dungeon in torchlight that had Jax and me wincing.

"...are they doing in *here*?" A sharp voice was saying. Female. Official-sounding. "Who authorized this?"

"Keradoc ordered the fugitives to be placed in custody," came the reply—a gravelly voice belonging to one of the guards who'd tossed us in here.

"No prisoners are to be housed on this level while prisoner 6712 is in holding," the woman said.

"But we were told to isolate them and—"

"Wait here and stay out of my way," she commanded. "I will deal with this myself, since you're obviously too incompetent to follow even the most basic orders."

Whoever this woman was, it seemed she outranked the lowly guard. I caught the outline of his hunched form as he nodded and stepped back, and then the door slammed shut once more, bathing the room in darkness and locking the woman inside with us.

Jax and I exchanged a glance. This was our shot.

The prisoner in the other cell tried to speak—6712, I presumed—but his words were weak and watery, and the woman ignored him. She headed right for us, her face shadowed, her every footstep echoing through my skull as I gathered my strength and prepared to—

Wait... No. It can't be. Is that...?

I narrowed my eyes, desperate to make out her features in the utter darkness, but I couldn't.

Not until it was too late.

She reached the bars of our cell. Peered inside.

"Holy shit," she breathed. "Saint? Is that you? And... Jax?"

Her violet eyes widened, and in them I saw the shattering of the fragile peace Jax and I had just managed to stitch together.

I saw the shattering of our bond, once and for all.

The demon peeled himself off the wall and took a wobbly step toward her. Wrapped his fingers around the bars. Gasped.

Then, in a pained voice that punched a fist straight through my chest, he spoke the name of the woman he once loved. The woman I'd sworn to him—on our very oath—was dead.

"*Oona?*"

9

ELIAN

"Oona," I echoed, not sure what else to say. Her name hung in the stale air like another corpse.

I still couldn't believe she was here. Now, of all nights, in all places.

I'd never trusted her back then—not until my final hours in Midnight the last time around. Before that, she'd been spending a lot of time with Jax, and I knew there was something fucked about her—just knew it. But he'd refused to see it.

So I followed her. Spied.

Took a few weeks, but I finally nailed her. Turned out she wasn't just some hot little blue-haired fae who liked to hang out at the pub in the Hollow and play Midnight card games with my demon brother.

She was military. Keradoc's Lieutenant General. And worse, his fucking daughter.

I wanted to kill her. Almost did, too, but she talked me out of it. Convinced me she really did love Jax, but couldn't escape her duty to the realm. To her father, despite his legendary cruelty.

Now, Jax continued to stare at her, his every cell already vibrating with the rage I knew was gathering inside him. I could practically hear it—the rush of blood, the thrum of his heart, the tightening of his muscles.

For his sake—and because I'd believed her—I let her live that night. Buried her secret deep inside, right along with everyone else's. And in exchange, she owed me. Perpetually. That was our arrangement, and it worked out well for both of us. She got to keep Jax and the illusion she was just another fae making her way on the mean streets of Amaranth City. I got intel on Keradoc and his officials whenever I needed it, and access to resources that would've otherwise been far out of my league.

Then, two years ago, Hudson's past came back to bite him in the ass, stirring up the kind of trouble that earned most people a one-way trip to the bottom of Beggar's Moat. The gargoyle never would've told me about it directly—rather than risk us getting involved and getting hurt, that sonofabitch warrior was ready to let himself be captured, tortured, and executed by Keradoc's men.

Lieutenant General Oona of Midnight got wind of the mission before it all went down, though. Knew Jax and I were close with Hudson. So she tracked me down, told me the story. Knew as well as I did the only way to keep Hudson's head attached to his body was to smuggle him out of Midnight and hide him in the earthly realm.

Getting out of Midnight was an impossible feat. No one had ever done it before. But with the right connections, help from the inside, and a good bit of forbidden magick cooked up by one terrifying dark goddess who'd been slumming it in Midnight recently, maybe we could beat the odds.

And, Oona reasoned, if I was going to smuggle out Hudson, I'd be taking Jax with me—those were her terms. Terms I happened to agree with. But we both knew Jax would never willingly leave her behind, and she'd never turn her back on her duty, so she couldn't go with us.

The only way then, she reasoned, was for Jax to believe she was dead.

A few nights later, when the plan finally came together, I knew we'd only have one shot to get out—one fucking shot. Me, Hudson, Jax. All or nothing. So, in my efforts to convince Jax he had no reason to stay, I'd painted the most grim, disturbing, hopeless picture my mind could craft, using my vampire influence and fae magick and everything I possessed to make him believe it.

It was quite a fucking performance.

Oona was Keradoc's daughter, I told him, pushing my influence deeper into his mind until the belief took root. Her father found out about their relationship—a daughter of Midnight fucking a lowly demon exile—and ordered his own men to kill her. I told him I'd witnessed it. Told him about the blood—so much blood. Told him about her strangled gasps as she supposedly died in my arms. Told him about my wasted efforts to save her, and how those same guards were after *him*, and he needed to leave Midnight with me and Hudson right fucking then or we were all going to be food for the ghouls.

I did not, however, tell him about Oona's demands of me. About how desperately she'd wanted Jax to have a better life, far away from the dark corners of the Hollow and her father's cruel regime. About why Hudson needed our protection in the first place.

"Why?"

It was only a whisper, but it dragged me right back to the present. Jax was still staring at Oona, and he didn't even turn to face me when he spoke, his voice soft with that quiet fury.

I'd never seen him so beside himself. Not even after I'd told him his woman had died, carved out his eye with a hot blade, and pushed him through the portal out of Midnight.

I opened my mouth to respond, but before I could figure out what the fuck to say, Oona was already talking.

"It was my idea, Jax. I begged him to manipulate you into believing I was dead so you'd leave Midnight with him."

"*Oona*." I shook my head, imploring her to shut the fuck up. Jax was going to hate me enough after all this—why saddle him with the burden of hating her as well?

"No," he said, as if he couldn't believe it. "No."

"It's true," she said. "It was the only way. I'm sorry."

He finally turned to face me then, his skin pale, his remaining eyelid twitching like he was T-minus thirty seconds from detonating.

"Why?" he said again, taking one step, then another, until we were nose to nose at the back of the cell.

Oona unlocked the bars and stepped inside our cell, but didn't come between us.

"I had an opportunity to leave Midnight," I said, forcing a steely calm into my voice I damn well didn't feel. "I wasn't about to leave you here."

"Why, Saint?" he demanded once more. "Why? Because you fucked up your life with Haley and you couldn't stand the fact that I found even a *shred* of happiness with a woman here? Or was it because you needed a demon lapdog to peddle your drugs and work behind your bar in New Orleans? Someone you could keep beholden to you for a fucking eternity, all because you let him believe you'd saved his fucking life?" He let out a bitter laugh, then slammed me against the wall, his fist wrapped tight around my throat. "You never saved me, Saint. All you did was drag me out of one prison and into another. I would've rather *died* that night."

Pain bolted through my heart. That's what he fucking thought? What he wanted?

That old devil dropped onto my shoulder again, taunting me.

Who gives a fuck what that asshole thinks? Should've left his ass here to die if that's what he wanted. Hell, there's still time.

"It was the only way to get you out, Jax." Oona placed a hand on his shoulder. "You wouldn't have left me otherwise."

"Damn right about that," he said, still glaring at me. "Because I—"

Loved you, he wanted to say, but didn't. I could just about taste the words on his breath, not that he'd ever said them out loud before. Fear demons weren't supposed to love, but I knew how he'd felt about Oona.

Knew how he felt about Haley now.

"It was the only way," she said again. "I wanted—"

"Stop." He finally released me. Turned to face her.

The dungeon fell silent once again. Even the rats had stopped squeaking, and prisoner 6712 seemed to be holding his breath.

Or maybe he finally died.

Oona tried to reach for Jax's face, but he jerked back from her touch.

"Say something," she whispered. "Please, Jax."

"Where is the witch?" he demanded.

Oona sighed, blinking rapidly as if she were still trying to put all the pieces together. "The Darkwinter witch? You know her?"

"Where," Jax said again, low and dangerous, "has your father taken her?"

Whatever she was about to say next, she swallowed it. Closed her violet eyes. Let out another deep sigh. When she looked up at him again, the confusion had cleared away, leaving only the grim determination of a soldier following orders.

"The Darkwinter blood witch is under guard on the top floor—he's put her in the guest suites. But you won't get far, Jax. He's got men positioned outside the entrances and on the balconies."

"Excellent," he said. "The more people I get to kill tonight, the merrier." He yanked a stake from the holster at her hip, whirled on his heel, and shoved it straight into my chest.

"What the fuck?" I sputtered, stumbling backward against the wall. I slid down into a boneless heap, the last of my strength abandoning me.

Oona spared one last look for Jax, then crouched down to help me. With a swift jerk, she ripped out the stake and pressed her hand to the wound, slowing the blood until my body started to heal itself—as best as it could, anyway.

The whole thing was over in less than fifteen seconds,

but those precious seconds were all the time Jax needed to make his move.

The bars slammed shut behind him, and he twirled a keyring on his finger—one he'd obviously taken from her. He also held one of her daggers.

Oona got to her feet again, leaving me on the ground. "Where the hell are you going?"

"I'm going to track down Haley, find a way out of this nightmare, and murder as many Midnight soldiers as I can along the way."

"What about us?" I asked.

"*You* can fucking rot." He glared at me, then turned that crazy blue eye on Oona. "Both of you."

He unlocked and opened the steel door. The guard Oona had argued with was still standing there. He had just enough time to reach for his weapon, but he wasn't quick enough on the draw. Jax slit his throat, then dumped the body inside, slamming the door on all of us as he slipped away.

Oona slumped down beside me on the damp ground. "Why didn't you tell him the truth?"

"You just said it, Oona. He wouldn't have left Midnight if he'd known you were still alive."

"No, I mean the truth about why you had to leave. About Hudson."

I closed my eyes and shook my head.

"It isn't my story to tell," I said, which was the truth, sure. But only half of it.

The rest of it I kept to myself—the part about how most of the time, it was easier to keep giving someone a reason to be disappointed in you than it was to carry the burden of his gratitude, or worse—the expectation that you could be counted on to do the right thing again.

That night, Oona and I had set out to save Hudson's life, and we'd succeeded. Whether Jax knew all the details was irrelevant.

She seemed to understand it—or at least understand that I had nothing more to say on that particular matter. With another deep sigh, she rested her head on my shoulder and pulled her knees up to her chest.

"Please tell me he at least had a better life," she said, the hope in her voice almost too much to bear. "Even just for those few short years you were out. Tell me what we did that night was worth it, Saint."

I said nothing. The Devil's Dream was finally kicking in, cocooning me in its familiar numb haze.

"Saint?" she prodded, lifting her head, and I sighed and finally looked into those teary violet eyes, and I knew —I *knew* she still loved him, knew she'd do it all over again if she thought for one *minute* it would give him a better life. Yes, even if it could only be better for a few short years.

I knew it because I'd do the same thing for Haley if I

could. The same thing for Jax, even if he kept right on hating me for it.

Oona nudged me with her elbow, but still, I said nothing. Not a damn thing.

Partly because I was finally too stoned to string together any more coherent words.

But mostly because I was locked in the dungeons of my worst enemy, blood leaking from more holes in my body than I could count, my soul as close to Death's door as it had ever been, and I couldn't bring myself to tell one more fucking lie tonight.

10

JAX

Keradoc's castle was as cold and black as the man's heart, a maze of damp stone passageways that twisted in all directions like tangled vines. Left, right, up, down, a confusing network no doubt meant to frustrate any would-be intruders and allow the lord of the manor to cower beneath his desk from a safe distance.

No matter.

I needed it tonight. The harsh, frustrating brutality of it all. Gave me something to focus on other than Saint's betrayal.

Oona's betrayal. Her rise from the fucking dead and her reappearance in my life at a time that was rapidly becoming its lowest point.

I wasn't sure which of them I despised more. Tough

call, but I'd meant what I said in the dungeons. After what the two of them cooked up together? They could both fucking rot.

Liar...

Dismissing that little voice whispering at the base of my skull, I pushed on. Right now, my priority—my only priority—was finding Haley.

Trusting Saint was a mistake I'd never make again—especially not when it came to her. When Saint finally found his way out of the dungeons, if he still wanted to assassinate Keradoc? Fine by me—I wouldn't stand in his way. But that motherfucker was on his own.

And so was his blue-haired co-conspirator.

Fucking Oona.

I couldn't believe she was alive. That Saint had so thoroughly lied to me that night. That Oona herself had been complicit in the act.

Fuck. Their treachery tore a fresh wound in my heart all over again, more painful than the still-bleeding holes from the devil's trap bolts. But as much as seeing her tonight gutted me, it also proved something. I wasn't in love with her. Not any more—and hell, maybe I never was. Not really. When I looked back on what we'd shared, the glimmer of my feelings for her felt like a pale, flickering candle compared to the inferno burning inside me for Haley.

Haley. Hold on, angel. I will *find you.*

I repeated the words in my mind, the mantra keeping me on track.

I didn't want to risk backtracking the same way the guards had dragged us in, but after a few more twists and turns through the damp lower levels, I managed to find a back stairwell. Judging from the musty odor and the thick layers of slime covering the steps, it hadn't seen much use —probably just the occasional servant or spy.

Back on the ground floor, I melted into the still-raging party crowd, my gaze finally zeroing in on a servant. Exiting the kitchens with a tray full of bubbly balanced on his fingertips, he was clearly heading up to the executive level; the rabble on the main floor didn't get their drinks delivered on silver platters.

I ducked into a shadowy alcove. Waited for him to get close enough to grab.

His neck snapped with an audible pop. Amid the chaos of the party, no one heard the champagne glasses shattering.

Two minutes and another dead servant of Midnight later, I was dressed in a tux just this side of snug, the black cummerbund fashioned into a sleek new eye patch, his silver tray in hand. After a quick trip to the kitchens to replace the drinks I'd spilled, I was on my way back upstairs.

With a brief nod, I acknowledged the guards monitoring access to the upper levels, sending out a faint pulse of generalized fear and uneasiness—just enough to keep them worried about their own bullshit instead of scrutinizing my half-assed disguise.

That's right, assholes. Nothing to see here. Just another poor chump serving drinks to the overlords of Midnight...

It took me another hour of dodging Keradoc's guards, searching the nooks and crannies, and climbing more twisting, turning tunnels and staircases before I finally found my way to the castle's topmost level—a massive gallery lined with dozens of oak doors that led off into what I assumed were suites and bedrooms, maybe a study or parlor or whatever the fuck kind of rooms the dark warlord of Midnight required.

The two guards positioned outside the doors at the very end were a dead giveaway, though—that's where Keradoc had stashed Haley. It had to be.

Still hidden out of sight on the landing, I tried to cobble together a plan. I had no idea how many guards were on the other side of the doors, but if I didn't take down the first two, it wouldn't matter. The doors were a good fifty feet from the landing. I couldn't just run over there, dagger drawn for a little slice-and-dice. They'd shoot me full of bolts faster than I could say *boo*.

Time to go old-school, then.

For all the humanity the devils of hell ripped from my

soul to turn me into a demon, the fact that they'd left me with a conscience was a fucking mystery. Guilt chewed at the edges of it now, but I ignored it. Took a deep breath and closed my eye. Blocked out all sense of right and wrong as I cast my awareness out into the darkness, searching for the one thing that could help me now.

And there it was. A whisper of fear slithering in the depths of memory. One of the guards had been betrayed as a young man. Tortured, brutalized, nearly murdered for his foolish, misplaced trust.

I focused on that ugly memory, tugging it to the surface of his consciousness until I felt the shift in his energy and knew he was looking upon his fellow guard with a suspicion that bordered on paranoia.

They didn't even argue. One minute they were standing side by side in front of the doors, hands resting casually on their weapons. The next, one guard stabbed the other in the neck, his body dropping with a soft thud as he choked on his own blood.

Still caught in the grip of his worst memories, the murderous guard darted down the hall, heading right for me. The closer he got, the easier it was for me to push into his mind, to mine the wounds of his past until he was nothing but a sweating, whimpering mess.

He barely noticed me as he blurred past at a run, then crashed through the stained-glass window at the opposite end, leaping to his death.

Thick rivulets of blood coated the remaining shards of glass. The sight was enough to unleash a flood of guilt if I let it, but I didn't. *Couldn't.* Getting Haley out of here was my only concern, and if I had to sacrifice a thousand Midnight soldiers to get to her, I'd do it in a heartbeat.

I headed for the end of the hallway, where the first guard's body lay in a lifeless heap against the doors.

Haley was just inside—I could sense her fear, tempered only by a fierce determination.

"I'm here, angel," I whispered. But just before I reached the double doors, they swung inward, and Haley stepped out.

The dead guard fell backward, landing at her feet. She startled and gasped, but I grabbed her and clamped a hand over her mouth, pulling her away from the body. Pulling her close.

"Don't scream, angel," I whispered into her ear. "It's me. Just me."

She sighed and relaxed into my arms, and I took a moment just to hold her. To inhale the sweet scent of her, willing it to chase away the blood and rot that stained my soul. The warmth of her, the softness, the aliveness... Hell, for a minute I almost forgot we were in this terrible place at all.

She was still dressed in her gown from the Feast of Midnight, though it was torn and filthy now, ruined with blood. Saint's blood. Mine. Hers as well, leftover from her earlier spells.

I understood that's how her magick worked, but the idea that she'd spilled even a single drop of her own blood for fucking Keradoc sent me into a fresh rage. It trembled through me in a wave, my arms tightening around her.

She finally wriggled free and looked up at me, her eyes flooding with relief.

"Jax," she whispered. "Thank the gods and the devil both, I knew you'd come. Where's—"

"Did he hurt you?" I blurted out, taking her face in my hands. "Did that monster put a hand on you?"

She sighed and bit her lip. Lowered her eyes. For a second that felt like an eternity, no words followed.

And for that split second of not knowing... *Fuck.* The very idea that he'd touched her made me wish I'd slaughtered more than just a few guards and servants tonight. It made me want to burn down the entire castle and everyone in it.

"Keradoc didn't... he didn't touch me," she finally said. "Not like that. He just..." Haley shook her head, her brow furrowed as if she couldn't find the words.

"You're not convincing me, angel."

Haley sighed again and lifted her hand, showing me a wrist cuff she hadn't been wearing earlier. Iron. I knew immediately what it was for.

"We'll get it removed," I said, hoping that was the worst

of it. "Right now we just need to get the fuck out of here. Okay?"

"Jax, when they first brought you to the throne room... You saw him, right?"

"Haley, we don't have time. We—"

"Just tell me what you saw when you looked at him. Please, Jax. It's important."

I blew out a breath. "Keradoc?"

She nodded.

"Black hair. Purple eyes. Soon to be a corpse, if I've got any say in the matter. Does that answer your question? Because—"

"Something was off though." Her eyes clouded, the wrinkle between them deepening. "I could've sworn he was wearing a glamour. And it looked like—"

"Haley, I will *gladly* analyze everything from his glamour to his hairstyle to his fashion choices to the twinkle in his fucking eyes, in whatever level of excruciating detail you wish, but not until I know you're safe and we're both far, far away from this fucking cage. Now take your pick of weapons from the dead guy, and let's go."

I finally got through to her. Her eyes cleared, and she nodded once before kneeling down to search the guard. Would've been great if she could've taken his uniform, but it was covered in blood. We'd have to figure out another disguise for her on the way.

She took his belt and holsters, along with a stake and

two daggers. "Damn. As much as I'd love to play around with that crossbow, it's too bulky to run with."

"Devastatingly sexy *and* tactical?" I couldn't help but grin. "I knew there was a reason I liked you."

"There are lots of reasons you like me. Now get us the hell out of here, sinner."

11

JAX

"Follow me, angel." I grabbed her hand and we headed for the gallery stairwell, keeping our eyes peeled for an ambush. I had no idea whether anyone outside had seen the jumper fall out the window, but eventually someone would find his body, along with his partner's at the end of the hall. Oona had said there were more guards posted on the balconies too—I had no idea how many, or whether they'd seen Haley leave her suite, but I wasn't sticking around to find out.

"Did Elian get out already?" she asked as we began our descent. "Do we have a rallying point? Do you know if he found Hudson? Shit, everything happened so fast before. And Gem! Where the hell is *she*?"

I said nothing, but she must've felt the uncomfortable shift in my mood, because hers changed as well. She slipped free of my grip and stopped on the stairwell.

"Jax." Her voice held a hint of panic. "Is Elian... Is he okay?"

"Far as I know."

"But where is he?"

My gut soured, and I muttered, "Rotting in the dungeons, which is a better place than he deserves."

"Wait... *What*? What happened? How did you manage to escape without him?"

"Oh, I don't know. Probably had something to do with me locking him in a cell and stealing these?" I retrieved the keys I'd stolen from Oona and dangled them in front of her.

"You locked him in a cell and *left* him there? What is *wrong* with you?"

"The list is long and sordid, and I'll enumerate it for you later, point by point. But first—"

"What about all that blood before roses stuff? We can't just abandon him, Jax!"

Oh, she was dead wrong about that. I could very easily leave Saint Elian to the rats and roaches of Midnight. After what I'd discovered tonight, there was nothing left tethering me to that bastard. No debts, no loyalties, and certainly no brotherhood. He'd pissed all over that bond the night he'd told me the woman I loved had been executed.

Blood before roses? Right. Those days were dead to me now. *He* was dead to me.

But Haley wasn't having it, of course. Snatching the keys from my hand, she said firmly, "Take me to the dungeons or tell me how to get there myself. I'm not leaving him."

Fuck. I should've seen it coming. Should've had some story cooked up in advance—we got separated, I lost him, he's long gone. Better yet, I should've told her he was dead, just like he'd told me Oona was dead.

Why the hell wasn't I a better liar?

I slumped back against the wall and closed my eye. Didn't matter what stories I invented. Haley could always see right through everyone's bullshit anyway. Mine. Saint's. Hudson didn't shovel as much of it as the rest of us, but if he did, she'd be the first to call him on it.

I waited a beat. Said nothing. My eye socket burned and itched behind the cummerbund, as if it were Saint's ghost come to fuck with me.

Seconds passed. Minutes. The rock walls seemed to be growing moldy around us, closing in tight.

"Jax." Haley broke the silence first, her voice considerably softer now. I couldn't decide whether that made me feel better or worse. "What is this about? I know you guys have issues, but this feels... different."

I shook my head, not even sure where to begin. "He lied to me about... about something he *damn* well shouldn't have."

"Oona," she whispered, and my eye shot open to meet

her gaze. Her eyes shone bright with sympathy, and she reached up to touch my face. "I saw her, Jax. After Keradoc brought me to the suite, she showed up with a report on Darkwinter's ships. You saw her too, I'm guessing."

"She found us in the dungeons. She was as surprised to see me as I was to see her, believe me." Fresh anger simmered to a boil inside, and it took some monumental restraint for me not to slam my fist into the rock wall. "He told me she was murdered, Haley. Swore it on our oath. It's the only reason I agreed to leave Midnight. He knew I would've stayed behind otherwise."

"He must've had his reasons for lying."

"Sure." My laugh rang hollow in the cramped space of the stairwell. "Just like he had his reasons for abandoning you and breaking your heart?"

I regretted the words as soon as they escaped my mouth, but Haley didn't flinch.

"I'm not saying they're *good* reasons," she said. "Only that Elian isn't... I don't know. He hurts people, Jax. Fucks us over in ways we probably don't even know about half the time. But he's not cruel."

"Does it make a difference? Someone stabs you with a blade, you're still bleeding—maybe even dying—whether they meant it or just tripped and fell in the dark."

Haley shook her head. "I have to believe he had his reasons for the lies, the abandonment... even if we don't know or understand them. And no, I'm not making excuses for him—what he did to you was a dick move. A *seriously* dick move that I'm ready to strangle him for on your behalf. But is that really enough to just... just leave him for dead?"

"You know what, angel? Yes. It *is* enough. You know why? Because I'm fucking sick of it. Saint's got reasons for everything—as many reasons as he's got pills, and I've been putting up with both for far too long." I turned my back and continued down the stairwell, hoping like hell she'd just shut up and follow me. We hadn't even reached the executive level yet, and I still needed to figure out how to disguise her from the party guests, dodge the guards, avoid another encounter with Keradoc...

But there was no angel behind me. Only darkness.

I climbed the few steps back up to her and reached for her hand. She didn't resist, but didn't move from her spot against the wall.

"I left him in the cell with Oona," I explained. "She's the lieutenant general. She'll get him out. The two of them will hatch some scheme, make their escape, and *very* likely find some other poor sucker to swindle along the way, but I'll tell you something, Haley. It's not going to be me. And it's not going to be you, either. So you know what? *Fuck* Saint. Let's go."

"We're *not* leaving him here, Jax."

"Sorry, angel." I shook my head. "I'm done. Done choosing Saint when all he does—all he's *ever* done—is choose himself. Every fucking time, every opportunity to do the right thing, he picks wrong. If the situations were reversed, he'd throw us both to the ghouls without a second thought."

"I wish that were true. It would make everything a lot easier, including telling Elian to fuck off for good." A sad smile curved her lips, a tear slipping down her cheek. "But you don't believe it any more than I do, so stop trying to convince yourself."

"I'm not the one who needs convincing. I'm..." I took a deep breath, tried to put Saint out of my mind. This wasn't about him. Not anymore. "Listen to me, angel. Everything else aside? I made a promise that I'd get you out of here tonight, no matter what. *You're* the priority here—for me and Saint both."

"Unfortunately, I made a promise too. Before we left New Orleans, I told you I'd have your backs in this place—all of you. I gave my word, and that means something to me, Jax. Even without a matching secret-society skull tattoo. So if you have that much contempt for Elian—if you're truly ready to turn your back on everything he ever meant to you, I won't blame you. But I won't join you, either." She turned her face and kissed my palm, then pushed past me on the stairs. "Tell me how to get to the dungeons, or I'll have to find my own way there."

"Wait," I said, blowing out a heavy sigh. "Wait."

I put a hand on her bare shoulder, and she stopped, her muscles tense, her hair tickling my skin.

"I'll take you to him," I said softly. "We'll get him out. But only if I can beat his ass later, and you promise not to interfere."

Without turning around, she put her hand on top of mine and squeezed. Then, in a soft melodic voice that lifted my spirits right out of the darkest depths, she said, "Jax? If you're beating that boy's ass later, not only will I not interfere, but I'll be the one cheering for you in the front row with a bag of white cheddar popcorn and a peach margarita, and *that* is a promise."

12

HUDSON

I wasn't one of them twisted fuckers who got off on pain, but when I finally regained consciousness? God *damn*, was I ever wishing for it.

Pain woulda meant I was still alive. Pain woulda meant my muscles and nerves still worked, and if they still worked, maybe I still had a chance at saving my girl.

But right now, there was only darkness and silence and a cold, empty ache where my heart should've been. My entire body was locked in my stone form, but it wasn't by choice. I couldn't shift into my warrior or human form, couldn't sense all the things I should've been able to sense as a gargoyle—where the fuck I was, for starters.

It meant one of two things.

I was either dead…

Or Marco's sunshine bullets were working some seriously dark mojo, keeping me locked up and helpless, just like the spell the fucker had used on me back in the day.

Either way, I had to keep fighting. Far as I was concerned? Marco was just another obstacle to overcome. Hell, not even Death himself could keep me from getting back to Haley, no matter how long it took.

So I did the only thing I could do. The only thing—in that moment of pure helplessness—that felt right.

I reached out to her. Called on our bond—something solid and real in this completely fucked-up realm of illusions and betrayals.

Took a while. Hours, maybe. No sounds, no sights, not even a whisper of a hint as to where those motherfuckers had locked me up. But then, out of fucking nowhere, I felt it.

A surge of pure panic. Haley's panic—same kinda thing I felt before, but way more urgent now. Desperate. *Fuck.* I had no idea how much time had passed since I'd seen her on the dais, but she was still in trouble.

Alive, fighting back, but in trouble.

And I was here. Not dead, I was pretty sure now. Just trapped. Ambushed by the same enemies who'd murdered my...

Fuck me. Tonight had all been a setup, just like before.

And now it was Haley's head on the chopping block.

The realization unleashed something dark inside me

—something wild and primal and just desperate enough to make me absolutely lose it.

Rage? That shit was my *own* form of dark magick, an old companion I kept chained up in the basement of the worst parts of my soul until I needed to set that motherfucker free.

Like right. Fucking. Now.

I pictured her. My mate. My woman. Thought of the warlord's hands on her, spilling so much as a single drop of her blood.

That old companion exploded out of his chains and burst through my chest like a bomb, colliding with Haley's magick, all of it amplified by our bond and my fierce need to protect her.

For the second time that night, I swore I'd died.

But no. I wasn't dead.

I was fucking free.

I was human again, naked, stashed in some cold, dark cave I didn't recognize. I quickly shifted into my warrior form. Stronger that way. Faster.

Way better for busting heads.

Marco and his fuck-faced little pals put a lot of trust in that magickal little gun of his. They'd only left two guards at the cave entrance—probably figured I wasn't going anywhere on my own, so why waste resources?

These assholes weren't even gargoyles, but vampires—I could tell from the smell of 'em. Standing around with their dicks in the wind like they didn't have a care in the world.

Why would they? Their prisoner was supposedly locked in a permanent stone coma.

My lips curled into a twisted grin. They weren't expecting me to find the motivation, but they'd obviously never met Haley fucking Barnes.

Good lookin' out, babygirl.

The bloodsuckers didn't even scent me coming.

I made sure they heard me though. Right at that last second. Stretched out my wings as far as they would reach in that cave and let loose a roar that burned my throat raw.

They spun around in a blur. And I smiled, more than happy to show them the face of their impending demise.

Fangs descended, but I wasn't in the mood for a tussle. I was in the mood to grab 'em both around the throat and repeatedly bash their skulls together until there was nothing left but the bloody stumps of their necks.

So that's what I fucking did.

Beautiful sight, that. Work of art, really.

I pitched the mutilated corpses back into the cave, then took off at a sprint, leaping out into the cool Midnight air as my wings fully unfurled behind me.

I was on the western side of the realm—some cave system in the Razorback range. The flicker of campfires dotted the mountainside, and I was pretty damn sure I could find Marco and the boys if I looked hard enough.

Pretty damn sure I could catch them by surprise and tear off their fucking wings—a fate far worse than death for a gargoyle.

I could practically smell the foul blood spilling from their backs. Hear their pathetic cries. It made my cock hard just to imagine it...

But vengeance would have to wait.

Haley was still in trouble—I could feel it now, stronger than ever.

So I took all that rage—centuries and centuries of it—and chained it back up in the basement.

Then I banked north toward Amaranth City.

Toward the woman who'd saved my life in more ways than one, more than ready to repay the favor.

Hold on, babygirl. Your Gargs is on his way...

13

JAX

"Get back," I whispered urgently, pulling Haley into the shadows of another corridor, shielding her from view of the guards.

Don't look, I muttered silently as they marched down the passageway perpendicular to ours. *Keep right on walking. Do* not *look this way...*

Haley gripped my hand and nodded toward the other end of our corridor, but that was a no-go. It opened back up into the main parlor where Keradoc's servants had been trying to corral the lingering party guests. The crowd had thinned substantially; our chances of being spotted were much greater now.

I shook my head. All we could do was wait for the guards to pass.

Only it wasn't just a few guards, we quickly realized.

They were transporting prisoners—three dozen or so, as far as I could count, made up of every race imaginable. Demons with glowing red eyes. Vampires, their mouths bloodied from a fresh feed. Wasted humans already well on their way to the afterlife. Shifters and gargoyles in chains, Hudson thankfully not among them. And fae, battle-worn and weary, their innate magick dim.

All of them wore armbands with the same black-and-gold insignia.

"Darkwinter," Haley whispered, and I nodded. Her heart beat so hard I could see the pulse of it in her neck, throbbing with every thunk of the guards' boots. "They're all wearing it. Even the non-fae."

It made no sense. Darkwinter fae were an exclusive bunch. Why the hell had they allowed the others to wear their colors? Their symbols?

"Where are they taking them?" she whispered.

I couldn't answer her. Not until I'd made damn sure Saint and Oona weren't among them.

Fuck.

Call it instinct, call it some twisted, misplaced sense of history. Call it fucking crazy, because I shouldn't have given a shit what happened to either of them.

But I did.

A red-hot bolt of guilt seared my gut, but then the last of the guards passed through without incident, and I smothered it.

Certain we were in the clear again, I blew out a breath and we slipped back into the passageway, continuing on in the opposite direction of the prisoners. If memory served, there was an exit at the end that led into the Sanctuary—a walled garden that hid a secret, underground entrance to the dungeons. The prison guards used it to sneak away during their shifts to score drugs and sex with the castle servants.

Saint, Hudson, and I had brokered many a Devil's Dream deal inside that garden.

I just hoped the entrance to the dungeons was still intact, and that any wandering guards and servants would be more interested in the party tonight than a clandestine roll in the garden.

"They're new captives," I explained, finally able to answer her question. "Keradoc and his men will probably interrogate them."

"And then what?"

"If they're following the typical Midnight protocol..." I scratched behind my eye patch and shrugged. "They'll likely beat the hell out of them, lock them up in close quarters, starve them for a few days, and then—when they're good and feral, rotting from the inside out, they'll load them into wagons and dump them over the wall."

"Into Beggar's Moat?" she asked with a horrified gasp.

"Ghouls gotta eat too," I said plainly. "Same as everyone else."

"But how do ghouls even eat?" she asked, her eyes shining with an innocent, naked curiosity that would've had me grinning if not for the morbid topic—and the fact that if we didn't find a way out of there, we'd be sharing the same fate.

Still, I answered her questions as best I could, if only to pass the time on our endless creep along the cold, black passageway. "It's a gruesome, terrifying thing to witness, and I pray you never have to see it, which gives you an idea of how bad it is because demons don't, as a general rule, pray."

She smiled, a ray of light in the darkness.

"When a body is dumped into the moat," I continued, "dead or alive, the ghouls are drawn to it at once. They swarm, fighting over the meat in their endless quest to consume. They know nothing else, Haley—just the frenzy of the feed. Then, when the last bit of flesh has been picked from the bones, and the marrow sucked dry, and every last drop of blood licked from the dirt, the ghouls fall to their knees and weep."

"They're begging," she said softly. "That's why they call it Beggar's Moat."

I nodded, a heavy sadness settling over me.

Midnight was a terrible place. I'd spent nearly two decades here and never had any false illusions about that.

But somehow, painting these pictures for her... It made

me see it in a whole new way. Not just as a terrible place, some cruel fate heaped upon even crueler monsters and men. But as… as a home. As a place like any other.

Stripped of its violent history and all the men who'd written it in blood, *every* place had the potential to be something different, something better… if only someone wanted to make it so. Decided it. Instead, Midnight's fae founders had turned a realm of magick and wonder and otherworldly beauty into a vicious torture chamber that left no soul untarnished, no heart unbroken.

I laced my fingers through Haley's and squeezed, quickening our pace.

"Is that where *all* the prisoners end up, or just the Darkwinter captives?" she asked.

"It's everyone, Haley. Everyone with the misfortune of getting caught committing whatever bullshit infraction Keradoc decides is a punishable offense. Could be you murdered someone, could be you smell a little funny that day, could be you're just breathing too much air in his presence. If you're unlucky enough to end up in the dungeons, you either die in a cell or you die in a fall over the wall. Either way, you're ghoul fodder."

She didn't speak for a long moment, but I knew what she was thinking. I could practically hear the wheels turning in her head.

"Saint and Oona excluded," I said, as if suddenly, after

all the ill will I'd wished on them both, I needed to hear it myself. "Oona's a high-ranking Midnight officer and Saint's —well, he's a snake charmer who can talk his way out of anything. As much as I want to set his ass on fire most days, I wouldn't have left them if I thought they couldn't escape."

"That doesn't mean they *did* escape."

I stopped and turned to face her, tipping her chin up until she met my gaze. "I *promise* you, angel. Saint is fine. I'm pretty sure this is a wasted trip—he and Oona are likely long gone by now."

She smiled, but it didn't quite touch her eyes. A hint of accusation still lingered behind them.

Fucking Saint. I really hope you're okay, you asshole...

And I did hope it, too. Not just for his sake, but for mine. Call me a selfish prick, but I didn't want to see that look in Haley's eyes *ever* again.

"Guess we'll know soon enough," she said, pointing ahead. "Look."

I followed her gaze to a welcome sight—the proverbial light at the end of the tunnel.

There, through a small doorway and a gate rotted with age and decay, two moons shone down on a tangle of vines, trees, and flowering bushes.

And—thank the devil—the garden was empty, just as I'd suspected.

"That's it," I said. "Come on."

With renewed hope, we headed out through the gate, stopping at the center of the Sanctuary before a towering fountain of two sculpted fae warriors, one carved of onyx and the other moonstone, their swords clashing in perpetual battle. Blood spilled from wounds at their necks, collecting in a pool at their feet, where it churned and bubbled in an endless dance.

"Is that... Holy shit, Jax. Is that real blood?" Haley stepped closer, but I stopped her with a firm hand on her shoulder.

"It's the blood of the realm. No one actually knows where the blood comes from, but it never evaporates, never freezes, never stops running. It's forbidden to touch or drink it—hence the vampire skulls." I nodded at skulls piled around the base, their fangs still gleaming.

Those fuckers always thought they could outwit whatever gods, goddesses, or entities haunted the realm of Midnight, but they never did. The moment the blood touched their lips, they died.

A shiver rolled through her body, and she rubbed her arms, chasing away the chill. "Where's this secret entrance? And please don't say we're wading through vampire skulls to get there. I'm really not dressed for an excavation tonight."

"No skulls, angel. Just a few plants and a little dirt." Still gripping her shoulder, I guided her toward the far wall covered in shadow and creeper vines. From here, it looked like a solid wall, but that was just the fae glamour.

"Ouch! Damn it!" Haley suddenly yelped. "What the *hell*?" She glanced down at her feet, stomping at some invisible assailant in the tall, leafy grass. "If that was a fucking snake, I'm out. Elian's on his own."

"Not a snake," I said, my heart leaping as I finally caught sight of the vines shifting on the ground. Panic gripped my throat, damn near cutting off my air. "Haley, listen to me. We're going down, and it's gonna hurt. You need to fight hard. Kick, punch, claw, whatever you need to do. Take a deep breath right fucking now and hold it or—"

"Wait, what?" Her fear spiked, sending my own into overdrive as the deadly chokeweed vines slithered around our ankles and up our legs.

"Hold your breath!" I shouted, but I knew the command didn't make sense, and there was no time to explain. The chokeweed swept our feet out from under us, dropping us flat on our faces as their sharp, golden thorns burst from the vines, tiny black blooms unfurling beside them.

We had seconds before those blooms released their toxic gas.

"Jax!" she cried out, swatting uselessly at the vines as they ripped into her skin. "What do I do? I can't get to my daggers!"

She was panicking, confused by the sudden threat. I

knew she'd fight hard no matter what, but there was only one way to fight chokeweed, and it wasn't with daggers or blood magick.

Fuck.

No time.

"Close your eyes!" I ordered. "I need you to trust me and close your fucking eyes right now!"

She finally did as I asked, no more questions, which made what I was about to do a hundred times worse.

I'm so sorry, angel.

Cupping her face, I called on one of her oldest memories—her oldest fears. I'd seen it the first time we kissed in that corpsevine field—her own mother trying to drown her—and now I drew it to the surface like I was drawing poison into a syringe.

I released that vile memory into her conscious awareness, amplifying it, making her believe it was happening right now.

In an instant she sucked in a breath and held it, then thrashed wildly, kicking for all she was worth. Her sharp, jerky movements knocked the blooms off the vines, neutralizing them.

Good girl.

I did the same, the thorns tearing through our clothes and skin, but unlike the poison, gashes were survivable.

After a few minutes of us thrashing around on the

ground, the vines finally receded, but they'd come back soon enough. They always did.

I got to my feet and hauled Haley up.

"What... what the fuck happened?" she panted and coughed. Blood slicked her arms and legs, and her eyes were wide with fright, like she still couldn't be sure she was out of the water.

"Chokeweed. Its thorns tear, the vines constrict, and the flowers release deadly gas. Only way to fight it is by aggressively shaking it loose, hard and fast. There wasn't time to explain. I had to improvise. I needed you to believe you were drowning. It was the closest thing I could think of and... Fuck, Haley. I'm sorry. I never would've put you through that if I thought there was another way."

I reached for her, but she flinched away at my touch.

"It's all right, angel," I said softly, guilt burning inside. If there was a medal for the number of times you could hurt a person in the span of an hour, I was pretty sure I'd win it. "You're safe now."

"Am I?" She glanced up at me, the terror still lingering. Then she closed her eyes. Took in another breath, blew it out slowly. When she looked at me again, those eyes were guarded. "Just... Look, I understand why you did it, but that was... Shit, Jax. You dug deep on that one. I need a little space."

"Haley, we can't—"

"Please. Just... I need a minute."

"You don't have one."

The chokeweed was already sprouting up again, creeping toward us like the fucking ghouls of Beggar's Moat in search of a warm body.

"We gotta move. Now." Without waiting for her response, I grabbed her arm and dragged her toward the glamoured entrance in the garden wall, but it was too late. The chokeweed covered the entire Sanctuary, new vines awakening with our every footstep.

"Fuck!" I lifted her off the ground and away from the vines, but no matter how hard I stomped them down, they just kept coming back. They covered the entrance, covered the wall, covered the fountain, slithering toward us like snakes. I might have been able to outrun them alone, but not with Haley in tow.

"What do we do?" she breathed. "What the fuck do we do? My magick isn't working!" She tried to call up a spell with her spilled blood, but that fucking cuff was muting her, and it fizzled out at the first flicker of light.

Still holding her in my arms, I smashed down more vines and tried to head back the way we'd come, thorns ripping at my legs, the tell-tale bright green gas drifting upward. We weren't going to make it. Not to the glamoured entrance, not to the old gate we'd come through. The vines were too thick, too strong.

"We hold our breaths," I said again. "That's what. And then we—*wait*. Haley, look!"

A dark shadow passed overhead, then circled back, swooping lower.

A shadow in the shape of a massive gargoyle.

I laughed, relief surging through my limbs when I recognized our long-lost brother. “Looks like we fly, angel. We fucking fly.”

14

HUDSON

Her fear was sharp and sudden, and it churned through me like acid, so painful it had me clutching at my chest and struggling for breath.

An icy chill gripped my whole body, shaking me like a rag doll. I was a hundred feet off the ground, yet I felt like I was drowning.

I pushed myself harder, faster, soaring right for Vanderham's Wall. There were no starshowers keeping the guards hidden in the towers tonight, and they were more than happy to use me for target practice.

Fortunately, they weren't as fast or determined as a gargoyle on a mission to protect his charge, and once I was over the wall and on the ground, it wasn't long before I lost them in the dank allies of Amaranth City.

Fast as I could on foot, I made my way to that fucking

castle, the bond an urgent, incessant tug. When a fresh bolt of terror rattled through my bones, I leaped up into the air once more, keeping an eye out for Marcus and his crew. My hope was they were off drunk or stoned somewhere, comfortable in the assumption I was locked up in that cave.

Cocky motherfuckers always made the best enemies.

High above the castle, I circled the grounds, my gaze roving over the last of the inebriated Midnighters stumbling home after gorging themselves in every way possible at the Feast. The taste of Haley's fear grew sharper, sharper still, until finally...

There.

I spotted them in the walled Sanctuary, Jax holding her close as he smashed his foot down on...

Aw, hell.

Chokeweed.

Motherfucker.

Stuff would cut you to shreds and poison you at the same time, just to make sure it got the job done.

I tucked my wings in close and dove down, pushing myself faster and faster until I had them both in range. Jax glanced up just in time to see me coming and lifted Haley up high. I snatched her out of his arms, then reached for him, but he shook his head.

"I'm going back for Saint!" he shouted, thrashing free

of the vines around his legs. "Get her out of here and stay out of sight—I'll find you in the Hollow. Gem can't be trusted!"

It was the last thing he said before he took off, fighting his way back through the chokeweed to that spot in the wall the guards used sometimes to sneak in and out of the dungeons.

I assumed that's where Saint had gotten held up.

Haley struggled for a minute, desperately reaching for Jax, but my girl wasn't stupid. No way could she fight through those vines—best to just let the demon do what he needed to do. The demon would be fine—we'd all tangled with the stuff more times than I cared to remember.

Just another one of Midnight's many fucking charms.

Eventually, Haley let him go, stopped squirming around, and held on for the ride.

I tucked her in close and zoomed straight up, getting us up to a good cruising altitude before leveling out again.

Two of the three moons hung high over the horizon, and I'd hoped to take a moment to catch my breath, check on my girl, and enjoy the view. But one glance ahead shot *that* plan to shit.

Dark shapes scudded across the moons, and a flurry of dark wings nearly blotted out all the light.

Gargoyles. Not the assholes from before, but Keradoc's

official team picks—bunch of bloodless mercenaries and sell-swords who didn't give a fuck whose heads they had to sever to make a buck.

"Incoming!" Haley shouted, and I banked a hard right, rolling to avoid a barrage of arrows on fire with purple magick. One caught the tip of my wing, tearing a hole right through it, but I ignored the pain and rolled again, narrowly missing another hit.

Fucking hell. Wasn't bad enough they'd sold out their own kind. They had to bring dark witches in to fight their battles, just like Marco. The whole lot of 'em seemed to forget what it meant to be a gargoyle. A protector.

Tightening my grip on Haley, I flew in a sharp zig-zag pattern as they fired another volley, the magick singeing my hide with another near-miss. I dropped down low, trying to lose them among the crowded, mismatched buildings of Amaranth, but the fuckers were relentless.

I circled back over the castle again, then headed north, wishing like hell I could fly us all the way out to sea. I glanced back over my shoulder. Counted. Six, as far as I could tell, armed and magicked to the teeth, ready to take us down.

"Hudson, the Fog!" Haley shouted, and I banked just before we hit the wall of deadly mist.

Fuck. I hadn't even seen it creep up. Shouldn't have even been there at all—that shit had never come so close to the city center before.

If she hadn't spotted it, we'd both be soup by now.

My gut churned with new worry. I had to get her the fuck out of there, and fast.

"Hold on, babygirl," I grumbled, then did a hard one-eighty, heading right back toward our attackers. I waited until they let loose another volley, then dropped into a free fall before zipping right back up again, trying to shake them loose.

I was heading for the wall. If I could get past the guards again, I could take her into the mountains. Or the woods. Or anywhere that wasn't the fucking city that seemed determined to kill us both tonight.

But good news apparently traveled fast, and as soon as we got near the wall, I spotted another squadron waiting on the ramparts, several of 'em perched and ready to take flight, the rest with their dark witch-enhanced bows drawn.

I made a sharp turn to double back, scanning ahead for another route. The way back to the castle appeared clear, but the new gargoyles were hot on our trail.

Seconds later, the original fuckers cut in from the east.

They were herding us back toward the castle, and there wasn't a damn thing I could do about it.

I tried to shake them off, to zig-zag again, to fly higher, but there was truly no escape—Fog of a Thousand Knives to the north, tower guards to the south, gargoyle mercs fucking everywhere.

Before I could even decide my next play, a burst of heat exploded across my wings. In a flash of purple light, a net of pure magick tangled around us, immobilizing me in midair.

We dropped like a hot rock, crashing down onto one of the castle's many balconies. It was all I could do to protect Haley from the fall, cradling her close as I took the brunt of the impact on my side. Pain ripped through my hip and shoulder, but adrenaline quickly chased it away as a dozen winged warriors landed soundlessly around us.

Two fae witches stood among them, just as I'd suspected.

And there, at the center of it all, was the warlord himself, his hair slightly windblown, cheeks flushed, as though he'd been standing out there the entire time awaiting our impending arrival.

Our capture.

"Are you fucking kidding me?" Haley shouted at the prick. She tried to stand up but I kept a tight grip, not wanting her to go anywhere near that bastard. Not as long as I could help it.

He leered down at us, his lip curled in disgust.

Never before had I so badly wanted to debone someone.

He didn't even bother acknowledging her. Just took one look, then turned on his heel and snapped his fingers, lord of the fucking manor. The witches stepped forward at once.

"Bring them to the war room with the other fugitives," he commanded. "And this time, when I tell you to secure them, I mean it."

15

HALEY

In a cavernous room on one of the castle's upper levels, Keradoc stood at the head of a conference table with his arms crossed over his chest, glaring down at us and looking supremely pleased with himself.

Gone were the formal silks from the party, replaced with an intimidating military ensemble that could only be described as Fuck Around and Find Out—The Dark Fae Collection.

All black, of course, and perfectly tailored to suit his lean frame, with a mix of soft leathers and hard, polished metals I was pretty sure didn't even exist on the earthly realm. Various pins and badges decorated his uniform, and nearly every inch of him was strapped with weaponry of the sharp and pointy nature.

A particularly stunning dagger hung from a holster at

his hip, the jewels encrusted on the hilt almost an invitation to grab it, jerk it free, and shove the blade right into his chest.

Somehow I resisted the urge, glaring at him with the daggers in my eyes instead.

He glared right back, fury simmering in that violet-eyed gaze.

Everything about him was spotless and precise—but for one thing.

His boots. They were covered in blood splatter. It was the same story with the rest of the guards who stood at attention behind him—more than a dozen fae, not counting another dozen on the opposite wall, and several who'd been left outside to man the exit.

Where the witches and gargoyles had gone, I hadn't a clue. Seemed Keradoc had a whole host of supernaturals at his beck and call; all he needed to do was snap those elegant fingers and issue a command, and they'd come running, guns—and magick—blazing.

I recalled the prisoners from earlier. The Darkwinter fae and their company.

Jax was right—Keradoc and his men had likely interrogated them. And in the end, when he'd wrung out every last bit of useful intel, he—

I swallowed hard, lowering my gaze once more to his blood-stained boots.

"Now that we've all gotten a live demonstration of what

happens when you try to escape," the warlord said, "I trust we won't be repeating the mistake. Is that a fair assessment? Or am I being too presumptuous? Admittedly, I wasn't expecting you to push things so far on your first night as my... guests."

One eyebrow raised in a perfect arch, he looked at each of us in turn.

Jax, still bloodied from the chokeweed encounter, his jaw clenched tight, rage radiating off him in waves.

Elian, pale and bruised and—if his blown pupils were any indication—tripping on the Black.

Hudson, still in warrior form, his wings bound to his back with iron bands that wrapped around his torso.

They were all draped in heavy chains spelled with fae magick so dark I could practically taste it, like burnt toast and ozone.

Keradoc hadn't bothered restraining me. Even if my magick wasn't muted by his cuff, he knew damn well I wouldn't make a move against him now—not while the guys were immobilized and Keradoc's backup team had tripled in size.

It was an intimidating show of force, but I'd seen his cruel side in the throne room. Seen what he'd done to those shifters for their so-called treason. The fact that the guys were still alive and relatively unharmed—even after our attempted escape? That told me *exactly* what I needed to know.

Keradoc needed them, just like he needed me.

The question was... what the hell did he need them *for*?

"Takes a real man to hold off on making threats until his enemies are all chained up," I said. "They teach you that at the Academy for Warlords and Supervillains?"

Keradoc bristled but didn't take the bait. Instead, he lifted a hand and glanced down at his black fingernails, sighing as if I were nothing but a petulant child. "Miss Barnes, do you have any idea what it costs me to keep prisoners alive in this castle?"

"Do *you*? I wasn't aware you kept them alive long enough to work out the financials."

A dark laugh slithered out from between his lips. "Fair point. In truth, I'd much rather toss you all over the wall with the dead as a reward for my ghouls. Alas, my priorities require a different approach." His smile fell. "I need you alive. *All* of you."

Just as I thought.

"What the hell do you want with us?" Elian asked, his words slurring. Jax still hadn't spoken, but the intensity of his gaze told me exactly what he was up to. Trying to find the chink in Keradoc's armor. Trying to mine his fears.

A shiver wracked my body as images of the Sanctuary flashed through my mind. The chokeweed. Jax's warm hands cradling my face, his touch calming me, like he alone had the power to save me.

Then, the water rushing over my head. The darkness. The cold.

I blinked away the memories. The old as well as the more recent. I was alive. That's what mattered. And so was my demon.

I wondered if a man like Keradoc even *had* fears. Jax believed the root of all fear was love, and he'd made a pretty compelling case for it. But if that were true, then he was out of luck tonight.

Keradoc was fucking fearless. Had to be. No love had ever touched that cold, dead heart. Not even his so-called daughter's. Of that, I was certain.

Unbidden, his earlier words came back to haunt me.

Kiss me like that again, Daughter of Darkwinter, and I'll be whoever you need me to be...

I sucked in a breath as the memory of that kiss, that passion swept over me, flushing my cheeks.

As if he could read my thoughts, Keradoc lifted that brow again, curious rather than authoritarian this time, his eyes glittering with something I couldn't quite pinpoint.

Intrigue?

I lowered my gaze back to his boots. The ones he'd probably used to stomp on heads. Because that's who Keradoc was—a cruel, murderous man-child who snapped his fingers and swung a sword whenever something didn't go his way. I refused to give that kiss—or him—another thought.

What mattered now was that the guys and I were together. Stronger because of it. We just had to figure out how to stay that way long enough to formulate a solid escape plan. Preferably one that didn't involve killer weeds or gargoyle archers or magickal nets or infuriating captors with deep, penetrating, violet eyes...

"As I've already explained to Miss Barnes," Keradoc continued, "I need her to craft and perform a ritual to summon her Darkwinter ancestors. The details are not important, but their resurrection will ensure our victory. The—"

"Darkwinter?" Elian gaped at me, some of the fuzziness clearing from his eyes. "Since when do you have Darkwinter ancestors? You're a witch, not a fae."

Shit. I'd nearly forgotten how far behind Elian was on the life and times of Haley Barnes.

"It's a long story," I said, "but let me give you the highlights reel of everything you've missed in Blackmoon Bay. Let's see... I've got three sisters. When we were little, our evil bitch of a mother murdered our father and tried to drown us because she thought we were trying to steal her magickal legacy, which all stemmed from this crazy prophecy about the Silversbane witches—four witches who would one day rise up to unite our kind against hunters and other oppressors and bring the sisterhood of witchcraft back into the light."

"Silversbane?" Elian asked, astonished. "You're talking

about the Silversbane prophecy? You... you're one of the four?"

I spread my hands and flashed a cheesy grin. "In the flesh. Descendent of one of the very first witches and—oh, you're going to love this part—her Darkwinter fae loverboys. Of course, this was before Darkwinter turned into the vile scum they are today, so I can't exactly blame a girl for going out and getting herself some of that hot, hot Darkwinter D, if you know what I'm saying."

I was pretty sure no one in that room knew what I was saying, but I smiled anyway. I had the Silversbane family tree to thank for my own insatiable appetites—a thing for which I'd always be grateful.

"Haley, that's... You've got sisters?" Elian asked softly.

Suddenly, he was looking at me as if I were the only other person in the room, his eyes shining with something I did *not* want to see there. Something I *refused* to see, because seeing it brought me too close to the past. To close to that old love, that connection, that closeness that had always come after we'd shared our most intimate hopes. Our stories.

He'd always known how important family was to me. And if he'd still been with me in the Bay, he would've been the first person I'd told after I'd discovered I had sisters. Real sisters.

"Sisters," I repeated, speaking over the tightness in my throat. "We were all born in Blackmoon Bay too. But after the attempted murder of four innocent girls, my granny—blood relative granny, not the Nona I've mentioned in the past—got with her coven and did some dark memory mojo to convince my mother we were all dead, then temporarily bound our powers, messed with our memories too, separated us, and shipped us off to be raised by new families, totally unaware of one another's existence. Granny happens to be the King of Hell's side piece, so obviously I didn't trust her story at first, but it turns out it was all true—it all came out during an epic battle in the Bay against the very Darkwinter fae dicks that are attacking Midnight. Seems they've got quite a hard-on for invading territories that don't belong to them. Anyway... yeah, you're looking at a super-special Darkwinter-fae-Silversbane-witch hybrid that our man K-Doc here believes can help him win his war against my own people. Aren't you sorry you ghosted me?" I laughed, then turned back to Keradoc, leaving Elian in shocked silence. Blinking up at the warlord with a faux-innocent gaze, I said, "Anyway, what were you saying? About why you needed the guys? As far as I know, none of *them* have Darkwinter ancestors."

Keradoc stared at me for a long beat, as if he was trying to figure out whether to laugh, run for cover, or just grab his trusty old sword and take my head off, nipping all that crazy in the bud.

In the end, he only sighed. Again.

It was a thing with him, I was quickly learning. The epic sighs.

"No, Miss Barnes. They do *not* have Darkwinter ancestors." Keradoc retrieved a small glass bottle from his breast pocket and set it on the table in front of Elian. Dozens of tiny black pills glittered inside. "*They* will be putting their talents to use on a weapon of a different sort."

16

HALEY

Devil's Dream?" I grabbed the bottle for a closer look. Elian's eyelid twitched.

"Unless my intelligence agents have deceived me," Keradoc said, his attention shifting between Elian, Jax, and Hudson, "you three are the men responsible for the current epidemic raging through Amaranth City."

"That's quite an accusation," Elian drawled. "Got any proof?"

"I'm well aware of your exploits in Midnight and back in your home realm." Keradoc rested his black-tipped fingers on the table, leaning close to Elian. "I'm well aware of how you escaped Midnight. I'm well aware of who assisted you, and I'm well aware of what those individuals received—*continue* to receive— as payment for services rendered. I've known all of it from the start, and I've allowed your operations to persist regardless of your status as fugitives and criminals, so kindly spare me the tedium of your denials."

Wisely, Elian said nothing. Jax said nothing. And—spoiler alert—Hudson remained silent as well.

"What I require now," Keradoc continued, "is for you to devise a more potent, more addictive formulation. One that will be spoken about in hushed whispers across the city, the mountains, and every last battlefront in the realm with an air of exclusivity and scarcity that will have the armies of our enemies clamoring for a taste—a taste we will gladly provide. While the demon and the vampire-fae devise and test the new formulation and my own soldiers begin feeding the rumor mills, the gargoyle will serve as my appointee in overseeing the harvest and transport of the corpsevine flowers from all known fields as well as any new territories we discover."

"You're trying to take them down from the inside?" I asked. "By getting them hooked on your dark fae crack?"

"A general must use every tactic at his disposal."

"Why not just poison them?" I asked. "Make them believe they're getting the good stuff, then... *wham.* Little black bottle of death."

"Darkwinter have powerful fae witches among them. Witches able to sniff out poisons."

"And you don't think this shit is poison?" I set the bottle back on the table. Elian shifted in his chair. If not for the chains, I was pretty sure his knee would be bouncing.

"Not in the same way," Keradoc said. "Dream is a recreational drug like any other. By the time the enemy soldiers realize the effects of its enhanced potency, they will be too weak to counteract it. Too addicted. It happens quickly, Miss Barnes." He gestured at Elian as if he were the newly appointed poster boy.

Just say no, kids. Be cool, stay in school.

"Dastardly," I said, unable to keep the disgust from my tone. "Another trick you picked up at the Academy? Bet you were the star pupil, weren't you?"

"Would you rather I—what's the term you use back home? *Nuke* them?"

"It *would* be faster," I said.

"Yes, and I suppose I have the magickal backing to devise a weapon of that sort. One that could take out the entire realm at the press of a button. The problem, Miss Barnes, is that whatever you think of Midnight fae, we do not—to borrow another quaint phrase from your homeland—shit where we eat. This is my *home*, for all that my enemies are attempting to claim it from me, and I do not wish to destroy it."

A glimmer of fierce pride shone in his dark eyes, and for a moment, I couldn't look away.

A strange understanding passed between us.

I knew what it felt like when your home was being threatened. What it felt like to want to defend it with your very last breath, by any means necessary.

The really fucked-up thing was... I could almost understand why he felt that way about Midnight. I'd only been here a couple of weeks, yet the place had already gotten under my skin. The thought of it falling under Darkwinter reign—under the reign of *any* enemy who sought to trample and destroy it...

Bile rose in my throat at the realization, but I couldn't deny it. Some part of me—a very dim, deeply buried part—actually wanted to help him.

And maybe, if he'd come to us with a proposal instead of demands—instead of soldiers and spelled chains—we'd be having a very different conversation right now.

"So your entire strategy for winning the war and saving the homeland you claim to love rests on the ability of four prisoners—prisoners you've already beaten and tortured, mind you—to remain loyal to your cause and carry out your orders without issue?" I laughed. "Really?"

"And here she thought you were the star pupil," Jax said to him. "Perhaps you need a refresher on your coursework."

"There is no such thing as loyalty, Miss Barnes," Keradoc said coolly, ignoring Jax. "Not in Midnight. But for the right price, certain insurances can be bought, and trust me when I tell you I've invested *heavily* in the ensuring of your cooperation as well as my own safety throughout our *entire* arrangement."

"What do you mean?" I asked.

"Let me keep this simple—for all of you—so there's no confusion later." He leaned even closer, his cold-roses scent slipping past my defenses, trying desperately to remind me of that stupid kiss. In a dark, dangerous voice, he said, "Should anything befall me or my personal guards, my generals, my staff, or anyone even *remotely* connected to me or this castle, your friends will be tortured while you watch. Should you attempt another escape, you'll get as far as the Sanctuary before you're captured and forced to torture one another for me and my guests, whom I assure you will pay quite handsomely for the entertainment. Do you sense a theme here?"

Yeah, I sensed a theme. Douchebag, with heavy accents of narcissistic personality disorder and toxic masculinity, framed in a neat little package of *complete* flaming asshole.

But I was pretty sure it was a rhetorical question.

I lowered my gaze and sighed. I didn't doubt Keradoc would hurt us. Badly. But he hadn't threatened us with *execution*, which further cemented my belief in what he'd admitted earlier: no matter what, he needed us alive.

His pathway to victory rested entirely on us—my spells, the guys' drugs.

Which meant we still had a bargaining chip.

No idea how much it was worth, but there was only one way to find out...

"Suppose we tell you to take your grand plans and fuck

off?" I asked. "Suppose we throw ourselves over the wall the first chance we get, sparing your guards the trouble?"

At that, his eyes widened a fraction, as if it hadn't occurred to him that we'd be anything less than compliant in the face of his threats.

Cards shown, asshole. Cards fucking shown.

"You've got demands," I pressed on. "You've stated them. You need me to do a ritual summoning. You need the guys to make a better, stronger pill to dose your enemies."

"Was something about that unclear?" he asked.

I folded my arms across my chest and shrugged. "Only the part where I tell you what we want in return."

"I do not take orders from captives."

A low rumble vibrated through Hudson's chest, but I smiled to let him know I was just fine.

"It's not an order," I said to Keradoc. "It's a bargain."

He laughed. That purple-eyed fae fucker actually laughed at me. "You and your pets are hardly in a position to trade."

I got to my feet and leaned forward, hands on the table, just like him. We were so close, our noses were almost touching. A ripple of unease moved through the soldiers on the perimeter, but Keradoc raised a hand, silencing them.

"Look around, Keradoc," I said, my voice just as low and dangerous as his. "Take a good fucking look at who you're dealing with here. You think the threat of pain scares any of us? You think we haven't endured our share of torture?" I laughed at the ridiculous notion of it. "Do you honestly believe you're the first asshole in my life who threatened to put his hands or weapons on me just to get what he wanted? Now, you may think I've got pull with Darkwinter fae, but let me tell you something, *sir*. Before I stepped foot in your realm, Darkwinter assholes and their human hunter minions kidnapped me, imprisoned me, tortured me, and killed people that I cared about. I've been stabbed, electrocuted, poked and prodded, starved, whipped, beaten, burned, cut, waterboarded, and those were the more pleasant abuses. Jax is a demon, for fuck's sake. You think you've got something on hell's torture chambers? Hudson doesn't even speak, so you can use your imagination on what happened there, but I'm guessing he didn't stop talking just because he lost a bet. And Elian? He's his own best torturer-in-chief, and the only way he can survive another day with his ghosts is to pop those little pills you're so ready to feed to your enemy. Now, tell me again how we're supposed to cower under the threat of *your* whips and brands."

Tension crackled on the air between us, my heart jackhammering against my ribs, Keradoc's eyes sharp with anger and mistrust and—though he was trying *damn* hard not to show it—raw, uncut lust.

As much as I hated to admit it, I was pretty sure he saw the same thing reflected in my gaze.

No matter. I refused to look away. Refused to back down. Refused to give a fucking inch on this—it was too important.

Through a jaw clenched so tight it damn near trembled, the warlord finally spoke.

"State. Your. Requirements."

"First, I need assurances my sisters will be kept safe. So whatever you need to tell Melantha to make that happen? Do it."

"Your sisters have nothing to do with—"

"The only reason I came here at all was to protect them. If they're not okay, *I'm* not okay, and if I'm not okay? I've got nothing to offer you."

"You seem to think I hold sway over the dark goddess."

"Don't you?"

"Melantha sent you to me in the hopes that I'd reverse her banishment and allow her to return to Midnight, which I cannot do. Very soon, word will likely reach her that I've captured her Darkwinter blood witch, yet I've made no move to commute her sentence. She will grant me no additional favors."

"Then send a *new* word to her that the witch you captured at the Feast wasn't me, but an imposter. Convince her that I haven't yet arrived—you're still waiting for your so-called gift."

"Miss Barnes. *Haley*..." His eyes softened a fraction, the tiniest flicker of guilt shining through. "Eventually she'll learn the truth. If Melantha is set on destroying your sisters, there's nothing I or anyone else can do to prevent that."

"Prevent it, no. But you can at least buy me some time to figure something else out."

"But that's—"

"Lasagna, Keradoc. It's lasagna, and it's what I need from you right now, whether you understand it or not."

He clamped his mouth shut. Closed his eyes. Muttered a whole string of curses under his breath, some in a language I'd never even heard before. The sound of it, even at a whisper, cast my whole body in goosebumps.

Goosebumps? Really? Since when am I the type of girl who falls apart over a sexy foreign accent?

"We're also going to need food, water, and clothing," I continued, straightening my spine and forcing myself to break free of whatever dark fae magick-mojo he'd obviously used on me. "And not the cheap stuff either. I can't be expected to work magick if I'm not comfortable, protected, and stylish."

"*Stylish*?" He scowled and shook his head, but when he finally opened his eyes again, there was no more fury there. The tiniest smile twitched at the corners of his mouth, there and gone again, but his eyes held the ghost of it, glittering mischievously beneath those dark lashes. "Very well. Will there be anything else, little thief?"

Beside me, all three of my guys stiffened at the sudden informality in his tone.

"One last thing," I said firmly, refusing to show him how that nickname, that tiny bit of teasing was already worming its way into my chest, trying to spark up a little fire that needed to stay cold. "I'm spending the night with my friends. *Every* night, actually, for as long as we're here."

With a laugh, he said, "Your friends will be sleeping in the dungeons, and trust me—the dungeons are no place for a woman. Especially not a woman whose spellcraft requires her to remain in top form."

"Top form?" I fisted his fancy, metal-tipped lapels and grinned. "Then I guess you'd better upgrade the boys to the executive suite, Keradoc, because along with fresh bedding, hot bubble baths, and green smoothies spiked with gin, your new favorite drug dealers are an integral part of my self-care regimen. So I suggest you unchain them, hand over the fresh towels, and escort us to those luxury accommodations, or you're going to find out why everyone says Scorpios are the craziest bitches in the zodiac."

17

JAX

I'd just settled into a steaming-hot bath in one of the suite's massive onyx tubs when she appeared in the doorway—my angel of darkness, freshly scrubbed and polished, damp hair piled into a messy bun on top of her head, some kind of short, black lacy little number clinging to her curves.

My heart almost liquified, though I couldn't say the same for my cock, now standing at full attention beneath the water.

"I should probably apologize for barging in on you," she said with a dreamy smile, "but I'm not actually sorry to find you naked and wet. Not. At. All."

"Nor should you be. Damn, angel. Aren't you a sight for sore—" I grunted as I sat up straight, taking in the sight of her smooth, unmarred skin. "—everything. I take it Saint healed you?"

"Yep. Vampire blood," she said, shrugging. "Hell—"

"—of a drug."

"Exactly. So why do *you* still look you fell into a wood chipper?" Her smile faded as she perched on the edge of the tub, her eyes scanning the mess of cuts and gouges on my arms and chest. "He promised me he'd heal you too."

"Yeah, well. Give him points for trying."

"Trying isn't doing."

I shrugged a shoulder, skimming my palms along the surface of the water. "He annoyed me, so I staked him."

"Jax!"

"What? It wasn't a lethal hit—just a jab in the thigh. Believe me, he had it coming."

"He *always* has it coming, but..." She swung her bare legs over the edge and dipped them into the water, toes gliding along my thigh. "You two can't keep going like this."

"Wanna bet?"

"You went back for him. You could've left the Sanctuary with me and Hudson, but you risked your life to go back for him."

"Don't read into it, angel. I told you I'd get him out, and I did."

"Did you see Oona again?" she asked, her voice softening to just above a whisper.

I nodded. "They were both still in the cell, but we split

up after I let them out. We all agreed it was best—couldn't risk her getting caught helping us escape. She's still a soldier of Midnight—our history doesn't change that."

"Do you want to talk about it, or...?"

"No, angel. I really don't." No point. It was all in the past now. A past I'd just as soon bury than drag out into the light for Haley or anyone else to sift through. "What I felt for her back then? It's gone. Even if she hadn't lied to me, I just don't feel that way about her anymore." I glanced up at her. "I'm not making any assumptions about what you feel or don't feel for me, Haley. But Oona's not someone you need to worry about. Ever."

"That's not why I was asking." Haley sighed and shifted her legs between mine, sending tiny ripples across the surface of the water that lapped at my chest, right beneath my tattoo. "It's just... You and Elian have this crazy-intense bond—it's so obvious you care for each other. Deeply. But then there's this huge wall between you, and I know it's not just about what happened with Oona. I can feel it, Jax."

"That wall took lots of years and lots of fuckups to build." I reached between my thighs and grabbed her foot, sliding my thumb over her arch. "Fuckups on both sides, as much as I'd love to blame it all on him. And a wall like that won't come down overnight—not even at the request of an *impossibly* stubborn blood witch with superior negotiating skills."

She laughed, the sound of it erasing all the cobwebs from my past. "I don't know about all that."

"Don't sell yourself short," I said. "It's no accident I'm sharing my bed with you tonight instead of with the rats and corpses."

"With *me*? Aren't you a presumptuous little demon?"

"You wouldn't turn down the last wishes of a broken, bleeding man would you?"

"No, I suppose not." She blew out a breath, her smile fading once again. "I hate that you're in so much pain, Jax. You should've let Elian heal you."

"Why don't you give it a try? I'd much rather your hands on me than his."

"I don't know how to do healing magick."

"But you *do* know blood magick, so maybe you're halfway there." I squeezed her foot. "You certainly can't make things worse, right?"

"That's a bold assumption, considering I'm operating at half-capacity." She rolled the iron cuff around her wrist.

"I think we both know I'm just looking for a reason for you to put your hands on me."

That got another laugh, and she shifted along the edge of the tub so she could reach me better. "Just tell me if it hurts, okay?"

I nodded, watching in fascination as she closed her eyes and ran her hands over my shoulders and chest, brow furrowed, lips muttering an incantation I couldn't hear.

Aside from the defensive maneuvers in Blackbone Forest and the throne room—both times when we'd been under threat—I'd never really seen her work her magick. Now, I took great pleasure in studying her face, the tiny wrinkle between her eyebrows, the way her chest rose and fell as her breath settled into a deep, steady rhythm.

After just a few moments, a soft, warm light emanated from her palms. Red, as her magick had always appeared to me, but fainter than before. Despite its lower wattage, it warmed me at once, and I felt my blood humming through my veins in response, following the call of her magick, encouraging the gashes in my skin to heal, the bruises to fade.

My pain receded, though whether it was more because of her magick or her touch, I couldn't say.

Eventually, the magick faded, and she opened her eyes and inspected her work.

"Holy shit!" A new smile broke across her face as she touched the now-smooth skin beneath my collarbone. "Does it still hurt?"

I shook my head. "Good as new, angel."

"I can't believe I just did that. I actually did that. I healed you!"

"Oh, I can *totally* believe it."

"You're just saying that."

"Angel, not an hour ago I watched you stare down the warlord of Midnight. You put the fear of hell in that man's eyes, and that's no easy feat. Something tells me there's a *lot* you can do that you haven't quite tested yet."

"Maybe." She trailed her fingers through the water, the ripples lapping at my skin. "Jax, listen. I wanted to apologize about before. In the Sanctuary? I'm sorry I snapped at you after the chokeweed thing. It just happened so fast, and I wasn't ready for it."

Guilt bubbled up inside, and I took her hand, pressing a gentle kiss to her palm. "You have nothing to apologize for, angel. I can't even imagine how frightening that must've been for you."

"You saved my life, and I pushed you away."

"I forced you to relive your worst memory—one your subconscious wanted to keep buried. You were terrified, and you had every right to be."

She didn't deny it. "Honestly, I'm still feeling a little... unsettled about it all. I only just learned about what my birthmother did recently. She found us again in the Bay. Wanted us to reconnect and join her fucked-up cause. My sisters and I... we banished her to hell."

She met my gaze, and I nodded silently. No one knew better than I did what banishment to hell was like. The fact that she'd had to do that to her own flesh and blood just to save herself...

It was an agony she never should've been forced to endure.

"Haley, I'm so sorry. You—"

She pressed her fingers to my lips and shook her head. "Don't say anything. I don't want to get into it now—not yet. I still haven't even fully processed what happened in the Bay. Right after that battle—after we sent my mother off—I had to leave my sisters to answer Melantha's call. The blood on my boots and daggers wasn't even dry yet." She ran her thumb over her wrist, tracing the words of her tattoo. *This too shall pass.* It seemed to steady her. "I'll tell you about it," she said. "All of it. I want to. Just... just not tonight. Tonight, I just need you to know that as scary as it was to relive my near-drowning, I'm not terrified of *you*, Jax. I never could be. Not now."

When I spoke again, my voice was dark and low. A warning. "Maybe you should be."

"Probably." She grinned, her eyes lighting up. "But I think we both know it's too late for that. I mean, it's kind of hard to be terrified of a demon when he's super sexy, naked in the bathtub, and you know the sound he makes when he comes."

Without warning, she slipped both hands beneath the water, trailing her fingers down my cock, which had been rock hard for her since she walked in. She fisted me and squeezed. Stroked, hot and slippery in the water.

"*Fuck*, angel," I growled, and she tightened her grip.

Every time the woman touched me, I lost my damn mind.

"Question about the drowning thing..." I ground out,

barely able to keep my voice even. "Are you afraid of water now? Of being submerged? Anything like that?"

"No, that's the weird thing. I *love* being in the water. I'm—"

I grabbed her and hauled her into the tub, cutting off her squeal with a deep, hungry kiss as the water sloshed over the sides, puddling on the floor around us.

"Jax!" she gasped, breaking away to admonish me. "Your injuries!"

"The strangest thing, angel. Suddenly, I feel like a new man." I kissed her again. "Guess you really do have the healing touch."

She pulled back and kneeled between my legs, bracing herself with her hands on the edge of the tub. The position gave me a perfect view of her breasts, her nipples outlined by the dark silk chemise that clung to her. I brought my mouth to her breast and bit, teasing and sucking her through the wet silk.

A soft moan, the slide of her fingers into my hair, the warmth of her skin as I ran my hands along her arms... If demons believed in heaven, I'd swear I was already there.

And maybe I could've stayed. Maybe I should've stayed, kissing her soft and slow, teasing her, making her whisper my name like a prayer.

But the silk in my mouth... it wasn't hers. And once that realization slithered into my mind, I couldn't let it go.

"What are you wearing?" I asked, pulling back.

"This? Found it in my fancy-ass wardrobe closet." She laughed. "Apparently, Keradoc took my demands to heart. Elian said some servants came to deliver a bunch of stuff while I was in the other shower."

"And you thought you'd give it a go, did you?"

"It's real silk. I'm not turning *that* down."

"That's not silk, angel. It's made from the petals of the Black Slipper—an extremely rare flower that grows in the Razorback Mountains." I rubbed the edge between my finger and thumb. The material was so finely woven, I could barely feel it.

If I could put a price tag on this flimsy garment in American terms, it would be in the six-figure range.

Keradoc was toying with her. Trying to lull her into trusting him. Liking him.

I'd seen the way he'd looked at her in the war room. Seen the bulge in his pants as she'd given him a piece of her mind, and I'd held my tongue.

But now, the idea of the warlord dressing her up like his own personal paper doll sent me into a fit of frenzied anger so hot, I was surprised the bathwater didn't boil up around me.

"He's trying to impress you," I ground out.

"Give me *some* credit, Jax," she said, frowning. "If Keradoc wants to impress me, he's going to have to work a *little* harder than silky pajamas."

"If that's how you truly feel, then you won't mind if I tear them off."

"Have I ever?"

With a deep, satisfying growl, I gripped the hem of the chemise in both hands and said, "Now would be a good time to heed my warnings, angel. Because I'm going to utterly *ruin* you tonight."

18

JAX

I ripped that chemise right the fuck in half, then made equally short work of the bottoms. They tore away like tissue paper, and I pitched the wet scraps over the edge, more than eager to welcome her naked flesh into my hands.

Her naked, Keradoc-free flesh.

Well, aside from the fucking cuff he'd clamped on her wrist.

Noticing where my gaze had landed, she sighed and said, "Don't even look at it. It doesn't matter."

"It *does* matter. It's like he's got a dog collar on you."

"Jax," she said, capturing my face between her hands, forcing me to look into her eyes. "Right now, in this bathtub, it's just us. *Nothing* else matters. Okay?"

She lowered her mouth to mine, and the taste of her kiss obliterated everything else—Keradoc's power games.

This fucking place. The drug mission Saint and I may or may not be able to pull off.

The complete insanity of our lives.

Haley was right. Here, now, there was only us. And nothing else mattered.

I stretched out my foot and twisted the faucet, replenishing the water we'd splashed out, filling the bathroom with steam.

Haley deepened our kiss, her tongue sliding into my mouth, her thighs clamping around my hips, my cock hard between us.

Our first time together, I'd taken her hard and fast in the woods near the corpsevine fields, where we'd clawed and bit and howled like animals. After that, I'd taken her hard and fast in the apartment. I'd taken her hard and fast in front of Saint, bold and brash as I pleased, and then on her knees in the shower. After that night, I'd taken her in so many other ways it made my head spin. My wild angel matched me every time, always desperate for each crazy, searing-hot touch.

Slow and soft had never been our style. But tonight? It was all I wanted. Needed. No, not because of my wounds—she really had healed me. But because being here in this fucking castle at the whims of the warlord I'd barely survived during my last tour of Midnight only reminded me how fleeting everything really was.

Tonight, I just wanted to feel her. All of her. One sexy, devastating inch at a time. And I wanted to make it last.

I broke our kiss and grabbed her hands, stopping her from fisting me again.

"Relax," I whispered against her throat, buzzing a trail of kisses along her warm skin. She was already resisting my hold, aching to get closer, to take, to receive. "Don't fight me. Not tonight."

"But we're so *good* when we fight, sinner," she teased, nipping my lower lip—a move that had me claiming her in another ferocious kiss, my hands sliding down to cup her backside as she writhed against me.

Fuck, I was so ready to just slide inside her and take her in every dark, wicked way, slow and soft be damned...

No.

I fisted her hair and pulled her back once more.

"Sorry, angel," I whispered against her mouth. "Tonight, you're *mine*."

Her eyes blazed with heat, with desire, with the pleasure of submission. She relinquished control, her muscles softening, her eyes dancing with curiosity.

I drew her close once more and brushed her lips with a soft kiss, then turned her around in my arms, settling her between my legs, facing away from me. Her hair slipped loose from the bun, falling in strawberry-scented waves, and I pushed it gently forward, baring her back and shoulders.

With a firm grip, I squeezed her neck, then slowly worked my way down to her shoulders, to the muscles between them, loosening the knots. She drew her knees up, resting her cheek on them as I continued to massage away the tension.

"That feels... amazing," she breathed. "You're turning me into rubber, which is awesome, don't get me wrong. But it's not exactly *ruining* me."

"Hmm." I kissed her shoulder, trying to work a particularly stubborn knot from her neck. "I'm merely softening you up so I can bend you to my every whim."

"It's torture. You know that, right?"

"What's torture, angel?"

"The way you're touching me. Teasing me. It's... God, Jax. Your hands are fucking amazing."

"*These* hands? These hands right..." I slid them down her back, down to her hips, then around the front, gently parting her thighs. "...here?"

"Yes, that's..." Her words trailed off into a moan.

"Lie back, angel. Close your eyes."

She did as I asked, resting the back of her head on my shoulder, her body stretched out before me. Her breasts peeked out above the waterline, and I blew a cool breath down over her shoulder. Her nipples hardened in response.

I cupped a handful of water, then poured it over her shoulder, watching it slide down between her breasts. My other hand snaked around her hip, dipping between her thighs again, a slow and lingering brush of skin on skin as I teased her clit with the barest pressure.

"Why?" she breathed. "Why are you still single?"

I laughed. "Fairly certain the answer to that question would fill up several volumes, not to mention completely kill the mood." I stroked her again, applying a little more pressure but keeping my movements slow and controlled.

Torture, just like she'd said.

From the bright flush of her skin and the hard points of her nipples, I knew she was enjoying every second of it. I slid a middle finger inside her, then drew back, circling her clit before dipping back inside, deeper this time, then out once more, every touch bringing her closer.

"I'm going to make you come now, angel," I whispered, biting her earlobe. "But I want you to remain *absolutely* still for me. Don't arch your back, don't tighten your muscles, don't even curl your toes. Just let it wash over you."

She murmured my name, her breath turning shallow as I stroked, my touch still so soft, so slow, until I felt the barely perceptible quickening of her heartbeat and knew she was right there.

Plunging my fingers inside, I finally brought her to ecstasy, and my angel did just as I asked, holding herself completely still in the water, my name a sharp gasp on her breath as the pleasure rippled through her body.

After a few silent, blissful moments, she finally turned

around again in my arms. Her cheeks were darker now, her damp hair curling around a soft smile.

I held her face in one hand and gazed into her eyes, black pupils swimming in a green sea.

"Every time I look into your eyes," I whispered, "I forget how to breathe."

Never before had I so desperately wished for the eye I'd lost. Wished for my full vision, so I could see every contour, every shadow as it was meant to be seen.

As if she could read my thoughts, Haley traced her fingertips along the edges of my makeshift eye patch.

"Let me see you," she whispered. "All of you."

I grabbed her wrists and shook my head, ducking her intense gaze. "You don't need to see all of me, angel. Trust me on that."

"Jax."

I didn't respond, shame burning through me. It'd never bothered me so much before—the scars, the mottled, caved-in flesh where my eye used to be. I'd gotten used to it, and there was no point in dwelling on shit that couldn't be fixed anyway.

But now, the thought of her seeing me... Finding me lacking...

No. I couldn't bear it.

"Jax," she said again, and I finally looked up at her again, everything in me suddenly wound tight with new fury.

It wasn't Haley I was furious with. It was Saint. Keradoc. This fucking place, and everything we'd done to stay alive here the first time. Everything we'd done to get the fuck out and try to start over in New Orleans.

And now we were back here, doing the bidding of a warlord who took pleasure in threatening the woman we both so obviously loved.

But Haley was the one in front of me now, soft and beautiful next to my hard, ugly, jagged edges, so she was the one who took the brunt of my anger.

"You really need to see the monster behind the mask?" I snapped. "It's that important to you?"

"Actually, yes. I do."

"I'm not your personal freakshow, Haley. If that's what you're looking for, take a walk through the Hollow. Plenty of freaks to choose from, most of them more than happy to show you anything you'd like."

"Is that what you think? That I'm just looking to satisfy some morbid curiosity?"

"Aren't you?"

"Jax, I already saw you without the patch in the throne room."

"I see. So now you just want a closer look? Trying to decide whether you can bear to look at it for however long this thing between us lasts? Or maybe you're ready to cut and run now, and you just want to make yourself feel better about—"

"Stop." The word was firm, but her touch on my face was gentle. "I'm not going anywhere, Jax. And I'm not trying to make you feel like you're under a microscope. That's not it at *all.* So keep it covered if that's what you truly want, but don't let it be out of shame or embarrassment or some fucked-up story you're telling yourself about what I'll think if I see you. I want you, Jax. Every bit of you," she breathed, kissing my jaw even as I turned away from her, shame still burning through me as sharp and hot as her words.

"I want every sexy line," she whispered, another kiss brushing my lips. "Every dip and hollow. Every scar, no matter how terrible."

Silence descended, hanging as thick as the steam in the air.

I turned back to face her. Held her gaze. Searched her face and knew she'd meant every word.

"It was my price, angel," I admitted. "My ticket back home."

A soft gasp slipped from her lips, but she'd done it—popped the lock off the vault—and now that those words were out, I couldn't stop the rest.

"It was Melantha," I continued. "She was in Midnight at the time. She's the one who cast the portal spell to get us out of here. So while Gem and the other Midnighters who'd helped us had their own price—a cut of our operations, which we'd be forced to continue in New Orleans—

Melantha had another. Money would never be enough for her, no. She demanded one thing from each of us—the most important thing, the thing that truly made us who we were."

"Your sight."

I nodded. "For a fear demon, our vision is what allows us to see into a person's mind and soul. To see their fears."

"So she just... carved out your eye?"

"She wanted me to do it, actually. But I... I couldn't. I held that dagger in my hands, the blade heated by fire, glowing red, and I just... I couldn't do it, Haley." I held my hands before her, both of them trembling at the memory. "I was damn near ready to shove it into my chest instead—just be done with it. But Saint grabbed the blade from my hands. Finished the job that I could not."

"Jax! Elian did this to you? He cut out your *eye*?"

"Not like that, angel. Saint did me a favor that night. There was no joy in it for him, believe me."

You hurt her demon, and I'll take the other eye...

Saint's old threats echoed, but I knew how badly that night still haunted him. He put on a good show, but half the reason we couldn't stand to be in the same room together was that most days, Saint could barely look at me. The guilt of what he'd done chewed him up inside; I could read it almost as clearly as his fears.

"Just... just take it off," I finally whispered, all my anger draining away. "If you want to see all of me, take it off."

Her fingers slid into my hair and stilled when she reached the tie knotted at the back. "Are you sure?"

I nodded, and she brushed another kiss to my lips, so soft and sincere I damn near melted.

With a gentle touch, she slid the patch over my head and set it on the edge of the tub.

It took me a moment to gather the courage to tilt my face up again. To let her see everything up close, the old wounds in all their gruesome glory.

I closed my other eye before I did, not wanting to see the change come over her face. The inevitable horror, or worse—pity.

I held my breath. Waited for the telltale gasp. The awkward stuttering.

But all I got was the tickle of her warm breath on my brow bone, her soft lips as she traced a path of sweet kisses along the ridges of my eye socket.

I winced, and Haley drew back.

"Did I hurt you?" she gasped.

"No, it's... Some areas are still a little sensitive."

"Elian couldn't heal you?"

"He did his best, Haley. But vampire healing isn't always a sure thing with demons, and... Well, this was about all we could hope for."

She traced her fingertip across my eyebrow, then down the long scar that bisected it, all the way to my jaw. "And this one? Did Elian do this too?"

"That one... That was *my* doing," I said. "After we left Midnight, I started having these nightmares. Migraines too. Melantha, this place... I never quite shook free of it. And every night I'd wake up with my entire skull feeling like it was on fire, and in those moments, I felt like I'd do *anything* to make it stop. Anything. So one night, delirious from lack of sleep and wild with rage and completely fucking devoid of all hope, I grabbed a dagger and I just..." I made a slashing motion, then shook my head. "Terrible idea, obviously, but when you're desperate and you feel helpless and you just... Fuck. Sometimes I feel like I'll never really be free of Midnight, even if we do make it out, and I swear to the moon and the stars, Haley Barnes, if you fucking cry so much as *one* tear for me over this, I will leave you here without a second—"

"Jax." She cupped my face, tilting it up until I looked at her again. "You survived. You're *still* surviving. So no, I'm not crying for you. I'm fucking *proud* of you."

She kissed me then, fierce and fiery, and wrapped her thighs around my hips, my cock hard between us, the water making us both hot and slippery. She was a survivor too, my angel, and had her own scars and stories to prove it, her own darkness to carry. And in that moment, I knew she understood me. Right down to my tarnished fucking soul. She'd seen it, and she was still here. Still in my arms. Still looking at me like she couldn't imagine a life where I didn't exist.

Without another word, she smiled and slid down over my length, taking me inside with a shudder I felt right down to my balls.

Fuck, this woman...

The bathwater was slowly beginning to cool, but in my arms, Haley was on fire, my angel of darkness and flame, burning me from the inside out. When she pulled back from that intense kiss, the darkness swirled in her eyes again, matched in intensity only by the bright light of her heart, a juxtaposition that made my head spin and my entire body ache for her in ways a demon shouldn't be allowed to feel.

For us, love should only hurt, like it had with Oona—a fae woman who'd allegedly cared for me enough to fake her own death to get me to leave Midnight, but not enough to trust me with the truth.

It should hurt, like it had with the men I'd once called brothers in a place where bonds were more often than not cast aside for a better offer.

It should hurt, like it had with my first family—the parents who'd condemned me to hell as a human, so certain I was a sinner beyond saving that they hadn't even bothered to try.

But Haley...

She made me feel almost whole again. Made me believe that it was even *possible* to feel whole again. And even as every warning about love and fear blazed through my mind, as my skull burned with old memories, as my chest constricted with old regrets, I couldn't help but feel this. But fall. But bring her closer to me with every deep thrust, every soft breath on my lips, every kiss. And when her eyes locked on mine and her body tightened around me and she came for me once more, my heart expanded in my chest, filling me, filling in the holes and gaps, softening the old hurts, muting the fears I'd so fervently fought against for so long.

"Jax," she breathed, and I swallowed her soft moan with another kiss—her lips, then her chin, then her throat, the sweet taste of her skin a fucking gift I still wasn't sure I'd earned. And when I finally came for her, it shook me right down to my bones, and I bit down hard on her shoulder, marking her with a silent promise as deeply as I'd marked her with my teeth.

A promise to love her the right way—not with the kind of false, fleeting, conditional love that hurt and destroyed, but with the kind that was *real*.

Now that I'd gotten a glimpse of it, I'd never settle for anything less.

We lingered in the water a bit longer, just holding each other, Haley humming another of her blissfully off-key, post-orgasm melodies—a sexy-as-sin lullaby that soothed me like none other.

When our skin had sufficiently pruned and the water had turned cold, I got out of the tub, grabbing a towel and one of the guest robes hanging on a hook behind the door.

But I didn't grab the eye patch.

I was done with it. For good.

"You coming?" I asked her, watching her naked form rise out of the water like a damned goddess.

"Soon. I'm just going to take a few minutes alone to finish up."

"Fine. I'll be waiting for you in bed."

"Whose bed, demon?" she teased.

"*Mine*. Also known as yours, since that's the only bed you'll be sharing for the foreseeable future."

"We'll see about that." She laughed, stepping out of the tub and looping her arms around my neck. "You're not ready to call it a night? Get some sleep before your mission tomorrow?"

Ignoring thoughts of tomorrow's mission, as well as thoughts of any other beds she might want to share, I pressed my lips to her warm skin and growled against her neck, the vibration making her squirm.

"It seems you misunderstood my intentions, angel. When I said I was going to ruin you tonight? I meant it. So no, I'm not ready to call it a night. In fact, I'm just getting started."

19

HALEY

Jax made my head spin as fast as he made my heart race.

Being with him was like climbing Everest and walking on hot coals and skydiving all in the same day—danger mixed with excitement mixed with raw adrenaline and an obsession that just kept growing inside me, every time we were together.

When I first met that sexy-ass bartender at Saints and Sinners, he'd intimidated the hell out of me. Now? Now he pushed me. Hard, then soft. Made me question my assumptions and challenge myself in ways I'd never bothered to before—ways I hadn't thought I was capable of. He made me want to stop running, to turn around and face my proverbial demons head-on.

And when things got to be too much, he brought me

right back from the brink with a seductive growl or a heart-melting kiss or the simple pleasure of a back rub that made me feel cherished and cared for.

Jax was a fear demon, a monster forged in hell who fed on the terror of others and had the power to bring people to their knees… Yet somehow, I was stronger and braver because of him.

And the sex?

Holy. Fuck.

My whole body flushed all over again, the ghost of his hands and mouth lingering, my nerves still buzzing with pleasure in all the places he'd so expertly touched me. Teased me. Claimed me.

But more than that—more than *all* of that—the way he'd trusted me tonight, the things he'd shared, the moment he'd finally lowered his guard and let me behind his walls…

When he left the bathroom without his patch, I knew. Right then, I knew.

I was falling for him. Hard.

And I was pretty sure he was falling, too.

The thought set loose a thousand butterflies in my stomach, making me feel light and giddy despite our current predicament.

After I finished up in the bathroom, I slipped into one of the thick, luxurious guest robes and headed out with every intention of joining my demon in bed, more than ready for Operation Ruination to continue.

But on my first night as Midnight captive, locked away in a massive stone castle carved by trolls, curiosity was an invitation I couldn't ignore.

Rather than heading back into the suite, I found myself padding out into the gallery hallway on bare feet, my heart thudding like it used to when I was a kid sneaking into Nona's kitchen for a stolen, late-night piece of her homemade tiramisu.

Back then, even when I got caught, it'd always been worth it.

Just a little exploring, I told myself now. *Five minutes, ten tops.*

The first three sets of doors beyond the suite were locked, but the fourth opened easily, revealing an impressive library larger than our entire suite, with rows upon rows of bookshelves. The back wall was curved, its towering windows offering a stunning view of the city.

There were no magickal chandeliers. No torches lit along the wall. Only the light of the moons and the flicker of red lightning on the horizon, illuminating the jagged peaks beyond.

Incredible.

I headed inside, slowly taking it all in. It reminded me of the city itself, an entire room carved out of raw black obsidian, a mix of smooth, polished-glass surfaces and rough-hewn edges jagged enough to slice through flesh.

Like much of the castle, the library was spotless and pristine, but it held a coldness to it. A darkness that had nothing to do with the absence of light and everything to do with Midnight itself.

The sight of it stirred something inside me—something beyond mere curiosity. With every step that brought me deeper into the room, my heart galloped harder, the hairs on my arms standing at attention. It felt as if the red lightning had charged the air, electrifying everything it touched.

Silently I crept along the rows of shelves, skimming spines etched with symbols and elegant script I couldn't decipher—probably an old fae language. I longed to touch them, to crack open their leather covers, but the last thing I needed was to open the wrong book and summon a demon—not the sexy kind—or unleash an ancient curse on the realm.

I continued on toward the curved back wall and found a reading alcove tucked off to the side, complete with a soft leather chair and a small table set with a flickering black candle. Beside it, a stack of old journals tipped precariously, the top one spread open.

A glass of amber liquid caught my eye too, and when I picked it up for a sniff, the ice inside shifted and popped.

Freshly poured, then. And—sadly—*not* the fae elixir I was hoping for.

Just bourbon.

I set it back down with a sigh, my senses picking up another familiar scent.

Roses.

Suddenly, Keradoc's scent was everywhere, charging me up like the lightning, the magick, the forbidden thrill of sneaking around in his library in my bare feet, naked beneath the robe, my hair still dripping water.

I took another deep breath of it, sickly sweet and ethereal, and tried to convince myself the sudden fizziness in my stomach was unpleasant.

I blew out a breath and shook my head, as if that alone could somehow shatter the invisible hold Keradoc had on me.

As if you really want *to shatter it, girl...*

Right. The voice in my head was obviously sleep-deprived, bordering on delusional, so I ignored it and focused instead on the stack of journals.

Careful not to disturb them, I crouched down and peered at the neat lettering inside. The entry was dated decades earlier, the page already starting to yellow:

Another setback tonight after the Parvaillian fae took the Towers of Wrath and Vengeance.

They felled my useless, gutless soldiers with an army of

undead, their necromancers stronger and more powerful than any I've ever encountered.

No matter. Soon those necromancers will bend the knee, and the surviving soldiers who failed me will know what it is to wish for a swift death.

In personal matters, Ashera has finally succumbed to her injuries, bringing an end to the experiment.

The child is inconsolable, clinging to me as viciously as the leeches of Hanging Lake. I know not what to do with her.

I fear she has inherited neither her mother's strength nor her intelligence, but perhaps that will turn out to be a blessing.

Those who lack spine and wits are much easier to break.

Tomorrow night, we send another company to the Towers to face the Parvaillians and reclaim what's mine. Should my soldiers fail me again, I will order them to march to the beach as soon as the Fog arrives.

—Keradoc of Midnight

"Holy shit," I whispered.

These were Keradoc's journals. Why was he re-reading them? Did he get off on revisiting his old tortures? His greatest hits?

And who were the Parvaillians?

Where were these so-called Towers?

And Ashera… Was that Oona's mother?

And what did he mean, "bringing an end to the experiment?"

Before I could read another word, a whisper of dark magick tingled across the back of my neck, the scent of roses thick and inescapable.

"Looking for a bedtime story, little thief?"

20

KERADOC

The witch startled at my sudden intrusion but didn't scream or gasp. She simply drew in a deep breath, turned to face me, and stood her ground, just as she'd been doing from the very first moment I'd looked into her eyes and demanded a dance.

"If wars could be won by lurking and skulking," she said, "you'd have every last enemy cowering at your feet by now."

"It's my castle, Miss Barnes. My right to lurk and skulk is practically written in the stones. Well, chiseled in them, anyway. This place *is* rather ancient." I tried for a smile, but as usual, she wasn't impressed.

"Is it written in your diaries too?" she asked.

"I know not. I was interrupted from my reading."

"Reading your own diaries." She clucked her tongue and shook her head, as though I should be ashamed.

"Wow, and I thought *my* Saturday nights were pathetic. Have you ever considered dating? Or maybe joining a club?"

"I wouldn't know the first thing about joining a club. I haven't participated in group activities since my Warlord Academy days."

She laughed. By the moons and stars, the witch laughed. But then, as if she'd been caught breaking some sacred oath, she schooled her features and cleared her throat, her gaze shifting back to the stack of journals on my table.

"Why *are* you re-reading them, anyway? Wait, don't tell me. Your therapist suggested it as a way to identify the lifelong patterns of self-loathing that led to your toxic, abusive behavior and complete inability to form intimate relationships?"

I had no idea how much she'd already read, but I didn't owe her an explanation or a justification. I reached forward and closed the open journal, my arm inadvertently brushing against her ribs.

She sucked in a sharp breath.

The unintentional contact sent a spark skittering across my skin, unleashing a barrage of memories I'd been desperately trying to ignore.

When our gazes collided once more, she shivered, then quickly turned away as though looking at me was a burden she simply couldn't bear.

My lips twitched into a grin. "The unexamined life is not worth living. Isn't that what they say on your realm?"

"Pretty sure pining over your emo-warlord high school diaries was *not* what Socrates had in mind." She headed for one of the towering bookshelves nearby, running her slender fingers along the spines of leather tomes that'd been shelved there long ago. Her hair fell in loose waves down her back, damp and curling at the ends, the wetness leaving a dark imprint on her bathrobe. My fingers ached to slide beneath the curtain of that hair, to discover whether the back of her neck would feel cool from the dampness or warm from her skin. Her magick.

The sight of that dark fall of hair, the wetness on her shoulders, the *very* recent memory of soft, shuddering moans echoing across the bathroom...

Her very presence tonight stirred an old longing inside me, like a bellows stoking a fire to life from ashen coals long presumed spent.

I could forbid it, of course. The cavorting. I could keep the prisoners separated, focused on their work, punished for any breach of whatever boundaries I chose to establish.

But eventually, I'd need to earn the witch's trust—enough to allow us to work together and see this mission through.

I'd met her demands thus far—provided food and clothing for her and her fugitives, set them up in accommodations fit for a family of noble fae. I'd even sent word to Melantha that I was still awaiting the witch's arrival, thereby securing the relative safety of her sisters for a bit longer.

Despite all of this, she still seemed unsatisfied.

She was more than demanding. More than obstinate. For all the fire she possessed inside, Haley Barnes was cautious, guarded, and—the trait most difficult to overcome—*discerning*.

It was a challenge from which I would not, however, back down.

I *would* earn her trust, whether it was warranted or misplaced, and I would do so sooner rather than later. Taking her away from the men she so obviously cared for—the touch she so obviously needed—would only hamper those efforts.

Besides, I'd be lying if I said I didn't take a good deal of my own pleasure from spying upon hers. Even now, the scent of her desire still lingered, her cheeks flushed from her very recent interlude.

"Where did you get all of these books, anyway?" she asked, stretching up on her toes to reach a leather-bound book of so-called fairy tales. It remained, however, just out of reach. "I didn't think a warlord would have time for pleasure reading."

"Most of the works in my library were smuggled here from your realm. Some of them are quite rare." I reached above her head and retrieved the fairy-tale book. "This is a first edition. The Brothers Grimm, if the name means anything to you?"

Her eyes widened with interest, and she reached for it, our fingers brushing. But that brief touch had her drawing back once more.

It shouldn't have irritated me, yet it did.

For fuck's sake, the woman had kissed me so passionately in the throne room, so eagerly, yet now she recoiled as if my touch might possess the power to leech the strength from her bones.

"You're welcome to borrow it." I held it out once more, but she was as defiant as ever, already shaking her head. "In any case," I said, "the library is yours to roam, should you choose. You may find some interesting occult or fae history books to aid in your ritual. But no lurking or skulking—*that* is strictly my province."

She cast her gaze to the chandeliers and sighed at my attempted humor. When she finally saw fit to look at me again, she crossed her arms over her chest and scowled. "How very Beauty-and-the-Beast of you."

"I'm afraid I don't understand the reference."

"Let me break it down for you. You're the beast in the equation."

Oh, you have no idea, little thief...

I reached for a lock of her hair, aching to brush it from her shoulder, but stopped short of touching it. My hand simply hovered between us, tickled by the soft whoosh of her breath. She gazed at it intently, mesmerized, and for a moment I wondered if she could sense the magick coursing beneath my skin the same way I could sense hers.

"I suppose that makes you the beauty, then?" I asked, lowering my hand and stepping closer. Too close. The scent of her freshly washed hair and skin intoxicated me.

"It makes… It makes me…" She blinked rapidly, then shook her head, ice hardening her features once more. "It makes me the prisoner, Keradoc. Nice clothes and soft sheets and a library full of first editions pilfered from the homeland doesn't change that."

I forced myself not to bristle at the rebuke. "Your stay here will be more pleasant if you stop thinking of yourself as a prisoner."

"I didn't come to Midnight for pleasantries, *warlord*. And even if I had, I wouldn't look for them here. I'm pretty sure you're not capable of anything even *remotely* pleasant."

"Your concept of what I'm capable of, *Darkwinter*, is severely limited."

"As is *your* concept of how good my imagination is."

"Oh, I've no doubt your imagination is rich and fathomless. So I want you to imagine this." I closed the very last of the gap between us and grabbed her arm, peering down into her glittering green eyes. "When you crawl into the bed of your precious demon tonight… When the others are fast asleep and he alone touches you… When he whispers against your pale neck... When he puts his warm, wet, demanding mouth on all the places that give you such wild and fevered dreams, I want you to imagine how it would feel to see him stripped bare, tied to the underside of the drawbridge, whipped until his very bones wept, and lowered into Beggar's Moat during the full triple moon when the light would grant the most *exquisite* view of the carnage. I wonder, *angel*, would he scream? Or would he hold fast, imploring you with that singular eye not to fear for him, not to mourn him as I sent his soul back to its eternal torment in hell?"

Tears filled her eyes, but she refused to let them fall. When she spoke, her voice was tight with emotion. With rage. "You're a *monster*."

"But not a fool." I released her arm. "Do *not* test me again, Miss Barnes. You'll not enjoy the outcome."

A flicker of fear danced through her eyes, mingling with a vile hatred that for some inexplicable reason made my cock stiffen.

Suddenly, I wanted nothing more than to bed that obstinate little witch. To fuck the hatred right out of her. To break her until she softened and moaned my name as she had the demon's, *begging* me not to stop...

We glared at each other in the flickering candlelight, another unspoken challenge rising between us.

I was tempted to use fae magick on her, if only to keep her in my company for the rest of the evening, to enjoy more of her sharp wit and my own dark, twisted fantasies.

But I wouldn't. Not now. Despite what she thought of me—despite the urgent ache in my cock—no, I wasn't the kind of man who drugged and manipulated women for my own entertainment.

I preferred to save *those* tactics for more important missions.

With a final warning glance, I replaced the book on the high shelf above her head and turned on my heel, leaving her alone in the library, trying not to chuckle at the sound of her soft grunts as she tried in vain to jump up and grab the book.

21

ELIAN

Fifteen minutes into our new gig, Jax and I were already at each other's throats.

Thanks to Haley, neither of us had slept much.

Jax, on account of making my little sparrow sing for him all night long.

Me, on account of having to listen to that shit, even locked away in my own sleeping alcove with pillows jammed up around my head and my heart slamming against my ribs and the thunder of a fresh storm rattling the windows.

On top of all that, the meager meal Keradoc's staff had prepared for us left us hollow and irritable—cold, congealed oatmeal and a few overly ripe pieces of fruit, along with a watered-down bottle of blood for me. Haley had taken one look at that shit, pushed up her sleeve, and offered the vein.

I was too hungry to resist, even though the sight of her made me want to jump off the highest turret.

What the fuck did she see in that demon, anyway?

And why the hell did she keep looking at me like she no longer wished me dead? Like she was actually glad I was here? It was my fucking fault we were in this mess in the first place. My fault for trusting Gem. My fault for not protecting Haley.

I should've been there to stop that fucking monster before he'd ever demanded a single dance.

Now, we were all caught in the same web, and I couldn't even kill him. Couldn't even try. One whiff of betrayal, and we'd all be on the torture racks.

Fuck.

When I'd had my fill—as much as I'd been willing to take, at least—I wiped my mouth with the back of my hand and said, "If you insist on sharing his bed, sparrow, at least stuff a sock in your mouth so the rest of us can get some sleep."

Yep. Championship asshole, going for the gold.

But every night that passed with Haley in my presence but not in my arms was another night some part of me shriveled up and blew away. Wasn't her fault, but still. It was better for both of us if she stopped trying to help me. Stopped acting like my personal blood bag and looking at me like she still cared—like I still deserved it.

When I looked into her eyes, there was still too much fucking hope there.

And hope, as she'd so eloquently told me that night in the apartment, was its own kind of poison.

Every night since, her words had echoed through my skull like a warning.

Hope? It's a drug worse than your Devil's Dream. A drug that causes delusions so powerful, you re-route your whole life around them until all you have left are the bullshit stories you tell yourself just to get through another day...

Now, trapped in Midnight, I didn't want any hope. Didn't need it. What I *needed* was another fix, but Jax's supply was limited, and until we could either make or steal more pills, I had to slow down—a task that would've been a hell of a lot easier if the bastard would actually tell me how much he was carrying, but he was keeping that card close to the vest.

It was all I could do not to trail him like a lost puppy sniffing after a bone, which sucked, because what I *really* wanted to do was beat the shit out of him for making Haley sing. Again and again. Fucking opera house, that suite last night. I wasn't surprised to learn Hudson had left early for the fields. Considering Haley was his fated mate, the poor bastard probably wanted to strangle Jax too.

So, after the meager meal and a well-deserved scolding from Haley, Jax and I left the castle, marching through the cramped streets of Amaranth City in hostile silence as we searched for our new job site.

We'd just turned down another dank, festering alley when out of nowhere Jax pounced on me, shoving me to the ground.

Two circular blades whizzed over our heads. We got to our feet and bolted toward the direction where they'd come from, but our would-be attackers were already lost in the crowd.

"Fuck," Jax hissed.

"What did you see?"

"Nothing. It was more what I felt—a spike of adrenaline."

"You think it was Keradoc's men?"

"I think there are plenty of people in this city who want us dead, and plenty more who want *anyone* dead, and maybe we just happen to look like easy targets." Then, giving me a quick once over, "You good?"

I nodded and scratched my head, grateful it was still attached to my neck. "Thanks for—"

"Old habits, Saint. Don't thank me." He shoved past me and stalked back down the alley, and I followed just behind him, trying to pay better attention to my surroundings. I was part vampire, for fuck's sake. *I* should've been the one to sense that attack. And if I wasn't going out of my mind about Haley, about those fucking pills, about all of it...

Excuses didn't matter.

Right now, I just had to get through this night. Check out our new work situation, figure out what we'd need to do to get Keradoc whatever drugs he needed, then make it happen.

"This the place?" I asked when Jax stopped in front of a low, squat building built into the side of a rocky outcropping. A few dusty windows lined the front, and I tried to get a look inside, but they were tinted.

"It's the address Keradoc gave me, so I'm guessing it's either our new office or a setup."

"Let's find out then, shall we?" With a grin, I pushed open the front door and stepped inside.

A bright magickal floodlight kicked on, temporarily blinding us as the door closed behind us with a heavy thunk. I'd just lifted my arm to block the light when four projectiles slammed into the door around our heads.

Not blades this time. Stakes.

Shot from crossbows.

Wielded by none other than our favorite purple-haired traitor.

Flanked by six guards, Gem stepped out of the shadows with a grin.

"Hello, boys. Miss me?"

I was on her in a flash, my hands wrapped around her throat. But before I could properly crush her windpipe, a painful electrical current surged through my body, dropping my ass to the ground.

Gem only laughed. "What about you, demon?" she said to Jax. "Want to give it a go?"

Glaring at her, Jax crouched down to help me back to my feet. My muscles were still twitching with whatever dark magick shielding I'd hit.

Fucking Midnighters.

"What the *fuck* are you doing here, Gem?" Jax ground out.

"Apparently, Commander Keradoc doesn't trust Elian not to steal the product," she said, "or you not to flee. So I've been assigned to supervise."

Hurt, rage, betrayal... all of it collided inside me, sending my heart into overdrive.

"Why?" I asked, my voice a broken whisper, and she knew damn well I wasn't asking about why she'd been put on babysitter duty.

Something dark and sad flashed in her eyes, but before I could make sense of it, she turned away from me and dismissed her entourage.

When she looked at us again, I saw that same sadness in her eyes and for a second I thought she might actually talk.

Instead, she shoved that crossbow into my chest and said, "No more questions, *Elian*. Now, considering you two already know your way around a drug processing facility, we're going to skip your orientation and get right down to business."

"That right?" I asked. "And what do you know about our business here, you fucking traitor?"

"I know I told you to stop asking questions. And I know if you two don't get to work, we're going to have a serious problem involving *my* boot up *your* ass. So move."

She shoved us ahead, steering us to a section at the back of the cavernous space where several tables had been set up for us, some of them holding trays of dried corpsevine flower, others covered with various pieces of lab equipment—beakers, test tubes, scales, burners, goggles.

There were other tables too—manned by fae and demons and vampires alike, all of them working on various stages of the production line: crushing the dried flowers into powders, preparing it to be pressed into pills, counting out and bottling the final product.

My mouth watered at the sight of so much Dream, but my infatuation was short-lived. There, on the far side of the space, were the testers.

Dozens and dozens of people of every supernatural race, all crowded together on the floor, all in various stages of delirium. Some of them scratched at invisible bugs crawling beneath their skin, others moaned through the pain of withdrawal, others trembled and twitched, desperate for their next dose. A few were stretched out on cots with IVs hooked up to their arms, concentrated black liquid dripping into their veins, their eyes glassy, their mouths open in a perpetual, blissful grin.

Several testers had already become corpses. No one had bothered to remove the bodies.

"I'll leave you to it, boys," Gem said. "But remember—I'm watching you."

Jax and I exchanged a look, then bent our heads to the work, rearranging the equipment until we had it optimized.

"Just like old times," I said.

"Yeah, except in the old times, our closest ally wasn't a fucking sellout."

I nodded, ready to let loose a barrage of curses about the bitch I'd once considered a friend, but something held me back.

The events of that night still didn't add up for me. If Gem had truly wanted to betray us, why did she wait until the feast? Why did she go to the trouble of getting us the apartment, the tickets to the feast, the formalwear, all of it? She knew we were heading back to Midnight, so why didn't she just have an ambush waiting for us on arrival?

And what was that look in her eyes all about just now?

"Jax," I said softly. "She keeps calling me Elian. Even that night after they shot us. She said, and I quote, 'it's like I always say, *Elian*... Nothing in Midnight is ever what it should be.' And just now she did it again—Elian."

"That's your name, asshole. How much Dream have you *had*?"

"That's not my name in Midnight. Gem only ever called me Saint."

His eyes widened as he considered the implications. "You think she's trying to tell us something?"

Another stake slammed into the wall behind us.

"Shut the fuck up and get to work, boys," Gem shouted across the room, "or the next one's going in your fucking skull. And don't think you're getting off easy either, demon. We're taking bets on who gets to pluck out that eye the minute you give us any shit."

I blew out a breath, my heart sinking into my stomach. "Guess that answers that."

22

HALEY

"How's things, babygirl?"

A deep, gravelly voice rumbled across the common room, and I couldn't help the ear-to-ear grin that stretched across my face.

Abandoning my latest failed magickal experiment at the dining table, I ran to my gargoyle, giggling like a schoolgirl as he swept me up in his powerful embrace, spinning me around.

"What are you doing here?" I asked when he finally set me back down. I handed over the notebook I'd started carrying in case he needed to scrawl out a message. "I thought you'd be out in the fields for another few hours."

He pushed away the notebook. "Starshowers closed us down early. Thought I'd come check on my girl."

I grinned again, loving the sound of that voice rumbling through his chest. He was in his human form now, fully clothed, his blond hair hanging in loose waves to his shoulders. I couldn't help but lean in for another hug, wrapping my arms around his waist and pressing my head to his chest. His heart beat strong and steady against my ear.

"So many words in one sentence?" I teased.

"For you? Hell yeah." He laughed, the rich sound of it reverberating through his chest, making my heart skip.

Hudson never spoke in front of the guys, and after everything that happened the night of the feast, he hadn't spoken out loud to me either. I didn't push him—just assumed he'd retreated into his old strong, silent protector mode.

But now, the first time we'd been alone together since he'd rescued me from the Sanctuary last week, it seemed he was ready to talk again.

And I was more than ready to listen.

"Hudson," I said softly, pulling back to look up into his chocolate-brown eyes, "what happened the night of the feast? I was so worried about you."

A current of white-hot fury swirled in his eyes—a darkness I'd never before seen in my sweet, protective gargoyle. "Ambushed by some fuckers from my past who ain't got no business calling themselves gargoyles."

"Ambushed?" My heart slammed against my ribs. "But... who? Keradoc's guards?"

"Not exactly. See, I knew something was up that night.

Saw Saint and Jax running off with Gem, felt like you were in trouble too. I searched everywhere, finally spotted you tied up in that throne room. But that's when they nabbed me."

He told me the story of the attack, the spelled bullets, how they'd imprisoned him.

"Oh my God," I gasped. "But... How did you get out of that?"

"Like I said, I knew you were in trouble. I could feel it. And I wasn't about to stay locked up like a statue when my girl needed me. So I got out, made my way back to the city, and found you and Jax in the chokeweed. You know the rest."

I shook my head, still marveling at him. I still had so many questions, though. How did he break that spell? And who were his attackers?

"And these... these guys from your past," I said. "They're... dead, I'm assuming? Hoping?"

Hudson laughed, but it was dark and hollow, like something scraping along the basement floor. "Yeah, babygirl. They're dead. They don't know it yet, but they'll get that memo soon enough."

"But—"

"Hey." He tucked a finger under my chin, tipping my face up as he brought his close. In a soft voice, he said, "I don't want you worrying about all that, okay? It's being taken care of. You got your hands full here, and that's a good thing."

"How do you figure?"

"Ain't gotta like what Keradoc's doing, but as long as he needs this spell, I know the bastard's gonna do everything he can to keep you protected."

"Imprisoned, you mean."

"Safe and alive, for as long as it takes for us to find a way out."

I nodded, leaning into him once more. Hudson wrapped his arms around me, so solid, so warm, and I sighed with pleasure. I didn't care how many walls Keradoc had built or how many guards he had watching over me. *Nothing* made me feel as safe and protected as a single hug from this man.

"Show me what you're working on," he said. "I'm feeling a little short on words now. I could use some Haley-speak."

"All right, Gargs, but you asked for it." Laughing, I took his hand and led him to the dining table, narrating my progress on the ritual prep in excruciating detail.

Rather, my *lack* of progress.

After our run-in in the library last week, Keradoc had pretty much ghosted me, which was just fine by me. The following night, I'd raided the library again, scrounging up a few books about Darkwinter history, along with some general texts on summoning spells and blood rituals. I looked for his journals, but no luck. After he busted me looking at them that night, I was pretty sure he'd locked them away for good.

So, for the next few nights, I read. Took notes. Ran a few small experiments—nothing too intense, considering I was still limited by the dampener cuff, but enough to deepen my understanding of how my blood magick might work in a summoning ritual.

My setup was pretty bare-bones, though—I needed some herbs and other ingredients, and I hadn't been able to find them in the kitchen. After the encounter with the chokeweed, I wasn't about to go traipsing through the gardens for a few clippings, either.

"You'll get there, babygirl," Hudson said now. "I know you will. And if you need shit from the city, just let me know. I can try to find it for you on my next run."

"Yeah?"

"Make me a list. I'll help you out any way I can."

I smiled, but the idea of it made me sad. Hudson and the guys had it way harder than I did, and there wasn't a damn thing I could do to help any of them. I didn't know how to make drugs, and I certainly couldn't fly over corpsevine fields and guard them from the many vicious creatures of Midnight.

It'd been less than a week since Keradoc had put us to work, and already the guys were exhausted.

Their nightly return to the castle at the end of their

shifts had quickly become the best part of my time here, because it meant they'd survived another day. That we'd be together under one roof for at least a few hours before we had to get up and start the grind all over again.

We always ate dinner together, no matter how late it was, and thankfully the food had gotten better—not quite as rich and resplendent as the Feast of Midnight spread, but an upgrade from that first day of cold, bland mush. I fed Elian my blood whenever I could—usually when he'd gotten too weak to resist.

But our conversations were short, all of us too wiped out for anything else. There was no way to avoid it—we all wanted to get the hell out of Midnight as quickly as possible, even if it meant working ourselves to the bone to make it happen.

Later, I'd tell myself each night as I crawled into bed with Jax, or sometimes with Hudson if he was having trouble sleeping. *Later* we'd have time for fun. For lively conversations over decadent meals. For stories told around a crackling fire about that crazy-ass time we all went to Midnight and helped the warlord secure another hollow victory.

Though they were all curious about my magick and the things I was learning each night, they never talked about their own work, and I never pushed the issue. What could they really say, anyway? They were making drugs. Testing them on people. Overseeing the harvesting and production of a substance that would ultimately—if Keradoc had his way—end the lives of hundreds of fae. Maybe thousands.

Fae whose same dark blood ran through my veins.

And yet, despite the cruelty of Keradoc's assignment, despite the regrets my guys carried about their involvement, there were times when I couldn't help but feel sorry for the warlord. All this subterfuge, all this violence, and to what end? Midnight had been at war for an eternity. Midnight *was* a war. What did he hope to accomplish?

And even if he achieved his goals and eradicated every last Darkwinter fae in the realm, even if he defeated every last rebel faction and claimed Midnight for himself once and for all, what then?

What did it mean to claim a place as your home if you had no one to share it with?

The thought sent a wave of goosebumps rippling over my skin, and I rubbed my arms to chase them away.

Even though I hadn't seen him, I could still feel the tingle of Keradoc's magick, still smell a whisper of roses around every corner. It always felt like he was watching me —even now—though I'd never caught him in the act.

"Hey," Hudson said now, bringing me back to the moment. "You got this. You know that, right?"

I returned his smile, bolstered by the vote of confidence. "You know it, Gargs." Then, blowing out a breath and glancing across the mess on the table, "I just have to keep experimenting until I get it right. I'm a powerful blood witch, for fuck's sake. Right?"

"Damn straight. And with all that Silversbane Darkwinter magickal woo-woo running through your veins? Hell, *I* wouldn't want to meet you in a dark alley."

I picked up a vial of blood I'd drawn earlier, swirling it in the glass, watching it cling to the edges.

"If my Silversbane Darkwinter woo-woo is so special," I said, "maybe the guys should be selling my blood instead of Devil's Dream. Probably get more money for it. Maybe we could just buy our way out of this mess instead."

"Your blood is not for sale, Miss Barnes." Keradoc's chilling voice echoed across the room as the warlord marched in uninvited. Then, plucking the vile from my fingers and replacing it in the rack on the table, "Your blood will turn our fortune in this war."

"My blood and your malice." I rolled my eyes. "Sounds like a winning combo to me."

"I've come for an update on your progress. In all this time, I do hope you've made some."

"Oh, and hello to you too, Keradoc! Hudson and I are doing just fine today, thanks for asking. And what about you?" I reached up and smoothed out the lapels on his impeccable military uniform, then tapped one of his many patches, which was probably completely disrespectful, but I didn't care. "Did you have a good night spilling the blood of your enemies and setting their puppies on fire?"

"Your *progress*, Miss Barnes." He reached up and fingered a lock of my hair. "Unless you'd like me to set you on fire as well?"

Hudson stepped between us and folded his arms over his chest, a warning growl rumbling through him.

"The skies have cleared, *gargoyle*," Keradoc said with a sneer. "You're needed back on the southwestern front."

"Hudson." I stepped out from behind him and glared at Keradoc. "His name is Hudson. And if you can't remember that, *fae*, you don't deserve to address him at all."

The three of us stood like that for a long moment, locked in a battle of wills.

Finally, Keradoc backed off.

"*Hudson*," he said—through gritted teeth, but still. "You're needed back at your post. And Miss Barnes, I really would like to understand what you've been working on. So, if we might continue?"

"We might, assuming you can behave in a civilized manner for at least fifteen minutes." I shot him a warning glare, then took Hudson's hand and walked him to the doors that led out to the balcony. Stretching up to kiss his cheek, I said, "I'll be fine, Gargs. Don't worry. Just be careful out there and come back to me in one piece, okay?"

He looked over at Keradoc once more, then back to me, his eyes full of worry.

"Go!" I teased, swatting him on the very firm, very nice

ass. "The sooner you leave, the sooner you can come home."

With one more warning growl for Keradoc, Hudson finally took off, heading out the door and leaping into the sky, wings unfurling behind him.

Reluctantly, I dragged myself back to Keradoc. "So. This is my performance review? Because honestly, I'm doing a terrible job. You should totally fire me."

Keradoc's violet eyes darkened, and he turned to look out the glass doors, hands clasped behind his back, his spine ramrod straight. "What do you truly know of this realm, Miss Barnes? That it's a prison? A form of hell? Or —what's the term you and your kind are so fond of—a shithole? Not that I can disagree with *that* assessment."

Looking out across the dark expanse beyond the balcony, I felt oddly defensive of the place. "If you feel that way about Midnight, Keradoc, why are you so determined to slaughter everyone who tries to take it from you?"

"Ah, but if it were that simple." He opened one of the doors and gestured for me to follow him out onto the balcony.

The air was cool, fresher up here than down on the streets, the din and squalor of the city muted.

"There are places on your realm," he said, "where beauty and riches are found not in what the eye can see on the surface, but in what lies beneath."

"Do you mean literally? As in gemstones and metals? Oil?"

He turned to me and grinned, his eyes twinkling in the moonlight. "All things the men of your realm pay great sums to acquire."

"Or to have someone else acquire for them." I glanced at the bloodstone ring on my finger, then met his eyes again, not wanting to draw too much attention to it.

"Or to steal it for them."

"Or they just declare a war and take it."

"Precisely," he said with a nod. "And so it is in Midnight. Only in our case, it's not diamonds or oil we're fighting for. It's magick. A magick that runs through every rock, every tree, every lake of blood in this realm. The magick of Midnight is a precious thing, Miss Barnes. Far more valuable than our cities and walls."

"Why are you revealing state secrets to your prisoner?"

"It's no secret. Not for the ones fighting to take it, nor the ones fighting to keep it. And not, I suspect," he said, turning to face me full on, "for you."

The intensity of his gaze made my skin burn.

"You're... right," I finally admitted. "I can feel it. There's a hum in the air—in the ground as well. More than a vibration. There's a palpable magickal energy here—sometimes I feel like I can actually *see* it. Like a phantom glow."

"It's palpable to *you*," he said. "Because you're a witch

with Darkwinter blood coursing through your veins. The magick of Midnight—dark magick—is your birthright. The longer you remain in my realm, the more connected to it you will feel."

Even as I blanched, his words sent a little thrill through my heart, making my pulse race.

But... no. Just because I had Darkwinter blood—severely diluted Darkwinter blood, considering how many generations ago my Darkwinter ancestors lived—that didn't make *me* dark. Didn't make me any more capable of harnessing and wielding dark magick than Hudson or Jax for that matter.

"I'm not dark, Keradoc. Not in the way you're thinking."

"No?" He crowded me, backing me up against the rough barrier that surrounded the balcony. "What do you see when you close your eyes, Miss Barnes? What do you find when you search deep in your soul, past all the things you believe make someone a good person, past the things you believe keep you safe from the dark?" He was standing so close to me now, I could feel his breath misting on my lips. In a soft whisper, he said, "When you sleep, little thief, where do the nightmares take you?"

He drew a fingertip across my forehead, his touch soft and cold, his magick whispering through my mind. It was the barest caress, but like Jax's fear demon mojo, this magick unleashed a flood of images so real I swore I could reach out and touch them.

Flame and shadow bending at my command, breaking the laws of physics and magick both.

Power surging through my veins, crackling at my fingertips.

Death rising, a thousand raw-boned corpses clawing out of the black earth and bowing at my feet...

I drew back with a gasp and shut my eyes, struggling to believe it. No, I didn't mean the visions themselves—those were as clear as the red-and-gold stars in the black sky, and I knew, somehow, they were real—as real as the fears Jax had brought to the surface to save me from the corpsevine.

Keradoc had just given me a glimpse of my future—that much was certain, even if I couldn't yet make sense of what I'd seen.

But the *feelings* those visions had unlocked inside me... How could I accept them?

How could I admit to the fact that rather than gasping in fear, I was gasping with excitement? With wonder? With hope that all of those things might one day be mine?

My whole body trembled with the possibility of it, and I clenched my fists at my sides, trying to calm myself. To bring myself out of whatever trance his magick had put me under.

"I... I should get back to my work," I said, glancing desperately toward the doors. Keradoc was still in my space, too close, too... everything.

"Yes, you should," he said smoothly. "But Miss Barnes?" He reached for my un-cuffed wrist, lifting it with a delicate touch, his thumb sliding across my tattoo. As I unfurled my clenched fingers, a black rose bloomed in my palm. Keradoc brought it to his nose and inhaled, unleashing a moan so lush I could've sworn he'd just come.

"Next time," he whispered, finally releasing me, "perhaps you'll think twice before passing judgment on my motives."

23

KERADOC

Hands and teeth as sharp as knives, he chased me. He always chased me. It was his favorite game. Refusing to play only made the punishment worse.

So I ran.

I ran in the dark. Ran through sharp-bladed grass that sliced my feet to ribbons, and I hid among barren trees that seemed to relish in giving away my position. They were nothing like the silver-leaved trees of home, the trees that cradled and nurtured and soothed.

These were the trees that burned and bled, and fed from the wounds of their victims.

Yet still, I hid behind them, just as he wanted me to.

And still, the wolf of Midnight found me.

He always found me, for it was his game, and it was as rigged as any could ever be.

Hands and teeth as sharp as knives.

"Don't struggle, pretty little fae," he said, his hand on my shoulder as he winked at me. "You'll only make me angry, and you know what happens then."

"My apologies, master." I dropped to my knees. Bowed. This too was part of the game, just like what came next.

A fist in my hair.

The sharp crack of a leather switch against bare skin.

Face pressed hard into the wet earth, his cruel hand as large as my head.

Gasping for every breath as he held me down in the rancid mud and took.

And took.

And took.

The pain, the blood, the darkness...

It crashed upon me in heavy waves, my screams muted only by his wicked laughter...

"No, stop! Please! *No*!"

I awoke with a start, heart hammering against my chest like the beating of war drums. Sweat rolled down my back, and my every muscle quivered in fear.

Nightmare. Just a nightmare. I was safe in the library, nowhere near the old forest. As for the wolf... the monster in the shadows had since been de-fanged. Now he rotted away breath by breath, bone by bone, no longer the master. No longer the predator, but the prey.

Don't struggle, pretty little fae...

I picked up the half-full glass of bourbon from my table. Pitched it against the wall. The clear, unmistakable sound of something breaking calmed my nerves.

I had no idea how long I'd been carrying on in my half-sleep, but soft footsteps on the polished floor on the other side of the bookshelves told me it hadn't gone unnoticed.

Haley.

In the week or so she'd been living here, I saw to it that our paths had rarely crossed. I preferred to let the guards keep watch, reporting back to me on the comings and goings of all my new guests. Being close to her was too distracting for me. Too dangerous. Too confusing, for the inexplicable pull I felt toward her had only intensified since that night on her balcony.

Yet I'd be lying if I said I hadn't watched her, on occasion. Hadn't lingered outside her door or peered through the windows of my own suite, hoping for a glimpse of her on the balcony, her long hair blowing in the breeze, her spine straight and determined as she looked out across the city lights, held out her palms, and tried to make her roses bloom.

"Keradoc?" came her soft call in the darkness now, as I

knew it would. I recognized the cadence of her steps as easily as I recognized the warm touch of her magick. The scent of her skin. All of it reaching me before she finally appeared before me.

She was dressed for bed, wrapped up in the bathrobe she'd seemed to so love, her hair woven in a loose braid that hung over her shoulder. In her hands, she held a steaming mug of peppermint tea.

"Are you all right?" she asked, her brow knitted with concern. "I thought I heard you shouting."

I felt as if I had one foot still in the land of dreams, the room blurring at the edges, her face as pale as an apparition.

"Something is... hunting me," I whispered. "A dark and vile thing."

The moment the words had left me, my thoughts cleared, the ridiculousness of my confession making the back of my neck burn with shame.

But Haley said nothing. No mockery, no sharp-tongued repartee about how I deserved to be hunted. Deserved to suffer.

Instead, with a look one could only describe as empathy, she handed over the mug of tea.

"Peppermint and lavender," she said softly. "I find it helps keep the nightmares at bay."

I thought to deny the offer, but the simple kindness

was a balm on my still-fractured heart, and I took the mug with a silent nod of thanks.

Her gaze locked on mine, she leaned back against the windowsill, the shape of her illuminated by the moonlight.

I closed my eyes and sipped the tea, grateful for the warmth as much as the excuse to look away from her.

"Thank you for the tea," I finally managed, "but I've no need of your company. You may go."

She shrugged. "Needs and wants aren't always the same thing. Besides, I'm feeling a little restless tonight too."

"Yes, well… As you can see, I've got plenty of work to…" I gestured at the book I'd left on the table—a collection of hand-drawn maps of the realm—but my weak excuse faded away in a sigh. "Why are you here, Miss Barnes?"

"I just came from the kitchen. I was on my way to my suite when I heard you."

"And?"

The compassion in her eyes deepened, the weight of it almost unbearable. "And… and maybe I know what it's like to be haunted by a past you can't even remember."

Her words struck a deep chord, and I couldn't help but wonder what was haunting her. Was it the mother who'd tried to drown her as a child? The sisters she'd never even gotten the opportunity to know?

Something knifed into my chest at the thought, but I dismissed it, chasing it away with another sip of tea.

"*Hunted*," I said softly. "I felt as if something were hunting me, not haunting."

"Is there a difference? Ghosts. Monsters. Memories. All of them can destroy us if we give them the power to."

"Power isn't always given away. More often than not, it is stolen from us. Stripped when we're at our most vulnerable."

"Then wielded like a weapon, keeping us cowed and fearful—yeah, I've seen this episode before." A heavy sadness touched her eyes, and in that moment, my own evaporated, replaced with a deep anger at the very thought of anyone wielding a weapon against her.

But then, as quickly as it had risen inside me, the anger vanished, hot guilt bubbling in its wake.

In my efforts to save Midnight, to pursue my own needs, I had done just that—taken her power. Wielded it like a weapon against her and her companions both.

Literally and figuratively.

Yet still, she'd come here tonight offering tea and a sympathetic ear.

Shaking my head at the wonder of it, I finally said, "It seems I've misjudged you, Miss Barnes."

"Hmm. You think?" A smile flickered at the edges of her mouth, and something deep inside me stirred, warm and hungry.

Longing.

The witch was getting under my skin in ways I should never have allowed, but it was happening, bit by bit, each night. Each moment, even this one.

When Melantha had first bargained with the Darkwinter witch, I'd been more than curious, more than eager to see how she might be of use. To see whether the summoning and resurrection of the Darkwinter ancestors really could turn our fortunes in this war.

In my mind, she was a means to an end. A weapon the enemy would never be able to defeat, just like I'd told her from the start.

But she wasn't just a weapon. She was a marvel. She was kind and generous. She was fierce and resourceful. She fought for herself, fought for the people she cared for. I wasn't certain of her combat skills, or whether she could even *hold* a sword, much less use it. But she was smart and quick on her feet. And she was powerful. In her presence, I could feel the threads of her magick even through the dampener cuff, the force of a thousand caged birds desperate to break free.

"Miss Barnes, I—"

"Haley," she said. "You need to call me Haley. Miss Barnes makes me feel like a naughty schoolgirl. Besides, I kind of like how it sounds when you say my name."

She shrugged like the admission meant little, but the dark stain on her cheeks said otherwise.

"Haley," I said softly. "There's something you should know. I never meant for you to… The situation in Midnight is complicated. I realize you and your companions feel like prisoners here, and in some ways, I suppose you are. But I do not wish you harm, Darkwinter. Only—"

"Darkwinter," she snapped, her eyes flashing, the momentary peace between us vanishing in a blink. "Your so-called enemy. The ultimate evil, right? Which is saying a lot in a place like Midnight."

"Haley, no. I didn't mean—"

"You *did* mean it, though. In your mind, that's what I am—an enemy. An enemy to be broken, bent, and reshaped to suit *your* needs. You've tortured those Darkwinter fae. Hunted them, just as they hunt you. So every time you say that name—every time you call *me* the name of your sworn enemy—you jam the knife a little deeper into my gut. So don't you *dare* tell me you don't wish me harm. The fact is, you *are* harming me. You can't just wish that away with some bullshit platitudes about how complicated your situation is. *Life* is complicated, Keradoc. Get over it."

"Midnight is at war—has been for a long time. I'm only doing what's best for my people."

"And who are your people, Keradoc? Your daughter? Your generals? The soldiers you leave to rot on the field? Or maybe the ones you parade through the streets until they finally succumb to their wounds? What about the people starving right outside this very castle, begging your servants for the scraps you've left on your plate? What about the people you feed to your ghouls?" She shook her head, a bitter laugh escaping. "If that's how you treat your so-called *people*, I'm happy to be your enemy."

My stomach churned and roiled. Every one of her accusations rang true.

But those daggers weren't meant for me. They were meant for the man whose mask I wore. Whose mantle I now bore, along with all the power—and the judgment—that had come with it.

I'd taken on those things willingly, gladly, all in service of my ultimate goal.

But when all was said and done, which of us would be called to atone for those sins?

Did it even matter?

I turned the ring on my finger, the skin burning and blistering beneath. It was getting more painful by the night; the magick was faltering, the bond between us unraveling. His death was close.

And mine was probably not far behind.

"I don't know why I ever thought we could have one nice conversation," she said, standing up to leave. "You know what? I hope whatever's chasing you in your dreams finally catches you, and I hope it bites off your—"

"Your sisters," I blurted out, desperate to defuse her. To make her stay, even for a moment longer.

To prove to her that I wasn't the monster she believed me to be.

Her face turned the color of the first moon. "What about them?"

I rose to my feet. "I wanted you to know that they're safe, Miss Barnes. Haley. I give you my word."

"And what, exactly, is that word worth? Can I trust you, Keradoc?"

"On this? Yes."

She held my gaze for a long moment, scrutinizing me through narrowed eyes, her breath stirring a strand of hair that had slipped from her braid.

Moons and stars, she was lovely. A dark flower blooming in an even darker world, and when I'd said I had no need of her company, it was a lie as bold and black as I'd ever told.

"I've got associates in Blackmoon Bay keeping a close eye," I said. "Your sisters are alive and well, as are the witches with whom they practice their craft and the men with whom they share their lives. A vampire and two demons, I believe? And a wolf shifter and a mortal man, or so I'm told? Honestly, the arrangement sounded rather tedious and confusing, but nevertheless, all are safe and well."

She pressed a hand to her heart with a gasp, and tears filled her eyes. "My sister Gray. Those are her mates. Asher and Ronan are the demons, Darius is the vampire, and

Emilio is a wolf shifter. Liam used to be Death, but now he's mortal."

"Death?" I couldn't help the curious lifting of my eyebrow.

"Long story."

"Indeed." I offered a tentative smile. "Such a strange realm, your home."

"You have no idea." She returned my smile, and it felt like forgiveness. "Did you mean what you said? Really? My sisters... Everyone's okay?"

"As I last heard from my associate earlier this evening, yes. Everyone is okay."

"Thank you, Keradoc," she whispered, her eyes glittering with tears. This time, there was no hatred behind them. Only gratitude. Only warmth.

She took a step closer and offered another smile, and for the briefest, oddest moment, I thought she might embrace me...

"*Haley*."

The gruff voice shattered the moment.

Elian. Her vampire-fae companion. The fugitive, drug-addled doppelgänger whom I still couldn't bring myself to look at with more than a passing glance, for every time I saw the face that tugged at my memories, Melantha's treachery burned anew.

She would pay. Dearly.

At the sound of her name passing through his lips, Haley's eyes filled with longing. Regret. Heartache.

And there, flickering around the edges, hope.

I hated him for it, though I didn't understand why.

"Be right there, Elian," she replied. Then, turning to me one last time, she placed her palm against my cheek and said, "Sleep well, Keradoc. Tomorrow is a new night."

24

ELIAN

Where's Jax?" she asked as we headed back into the common room.

Of course that would be the first question out of her mouth.

"Don't know, don't care. I'm more concerned about what you're doing having tea with our jailor like you're old chums."

Haley laughed. "Seriously, Elian? I think we've got *slightly* bigger issues to worry about than who's attending afternoon tea. I mean evening tea. Or... whatever the hell time it is. Either way, I'm beat, so I'm going to bed."

Pushing past me, she headed for her bedroom.

Jax's bedroom.

Fuck. Even when he wasn't home, she still wanted to be close to him.

Jealousy, that old friend, burned through my gut as I

watched her remove her robe and strip down to nothing but a thin T-shirt and panties.

She crawled beneath the blankets, then glared at me. "Um, you here to tuck me in, or...?"

In response, I took a seat in the chair beside the bed. Folded my hands in my lap. Smiled. "Just keeping an eye on you, little sparrow. Since your boyfriend can't be bothered."

She rolled her pretty green eyes and punched down her pillow, then settled in with a sigh. "You can stay as long as you want, Elian, but only if you promise not to be a dick."

"Can't promise I won't *be* a dick, but I'll do my best to hide my true nature."

This got a smile. "Fair enough. So... what's on your mind?"

"Nothing, I... I just thought maybe we could... talk?"

"Talk? About what?"

I leaned forward, watching her in the light of the triple moons that shone through the window, searching through my fractured mind for a safe topic—one that wouldn't send me into a jealous rage or cause her to kick my ass out.

There was no real purpose for my visit. Only that Jax and Hudson weren't here, and it was the first time I'd been alone with her since that night in the apartment—the night Jax had made her come with my name on her lips—and I just... I needed to be with her.

And this was the only way.

Talking.

"You have sisters," I said finally.

Her eyes softened, a sweet smile touching her lips. "Gray, Georgie, and Adele."

"And you. The four Silversbane witches," I said, remembering what she'd told me in Keradoc's war room that night. "I still can't wrap my head around it. You're part of the prophecy—that's insane, Haley. I'd always assumed it was a legend."

"Nope. You're in the presence of greatness," she teased. "Practically witch-fae royalty right here. Maybe you should kiss my feet." She stuck a foot out from under the blanket and nudged my knee.

I grabbed it, gave it a squeeze. Held it, soft and warm in my hand, unable—unwilling—to let go.

The playfulness in her eyes shifted to something more serious, and in them I saw a deep longing I wanted nothing more than to dive right into.

"Haley," I whispered, and she bit her lip and lowered her gaze, pulling her foot out of my grasp.

"Elian, I… I'm…" She sighed, and I was already feeling the crushing weight of her rejection, knowing she was about to kick me out.

Probably for the best.

But then she scooted over to the side of the bed, looked up at me again, and patted the empty space next to her.

I didn't move.

"Just for a little while," she said softly. "Please? Yes, I know I'm needy and whiny and impossible, but—"

"You know I can't say no to you, little sparrow." I rose from the chair. "You sure your boyfriend won't get mad if he comes home and finds me in bed with his woman?" I teased, but I was already sliding in next to her.

Like I gave a fuck what Jax would think. It was his fault for not being here.

That's right, asshole, the little voice inside my head said. *She was* your *girl first. Just because you can't fuck her doesn't mean you can't* think *about fucking her. Doesn't mean you can't lay next to her and remember what it was like...*

Ignoring the pulse of heat in my cock, I settled in next to her, rolling onto my hip to face her. The bed was warm from her body, the moonlight painting her face, and for a long moment I just... watched her. Drank her in. Tried to set aside my complicated feelings and the pain and the regrets and all the fucked-up shit between us and just appreciate the fact that for right now, whether it would be for an hour or fifteen seconds, I had her all to myself.

I didn't even care that we'd stopped talking. Just being here, just looking at her was enough.

But then she reached up to touch one of my silver braids, and sadness washed through her eyes, her mouth pulling into a frown.

"Elian," she whispered, and I held my breath, knowing

—just fucking *knowing*—what would come next. "Who's Evander?"

A smile touched my lips, but then it vanished, swallowed up by the ache inside me that would never heal.

"You used to dream about him," she continued softly, as if I could ever forget. As if I didn't *still* dream about him, didn't still see him every time I closed my eyes. "Back in the Bay sometimes. I remember you'd—"

"I know, sparrow. It… it was a long time ago."

"That night in the throne room, though… What made you think of him?"

I didn't answer her. Couldn't. The truth still sounded too fucking crazy, even in my own drug-addled brain—a place that practically thrived on crazy.

"Is Evander the reason you…" She trailed off into a sigh, then lifted her other hand, the unmistakable black pill pinched between her thumb and forefinger.

"Haley!" I bolted upright and leaned over her, trying to take it. "Where did you get that?"

She closed her fist around it and shrugged. "I found it in the kitchen. One of the staff probably dropped it."

"Give it to me."

Still clutching it in her fist, she said, "What does it feel like? I used to turn my nose up at the idea of trying it, but I have to admit—I'm kind of curious now."

"Please, sparrow," I whispered, tracing a soft line down

her cheek. "You don't want to get mixed up with the Devil —trust me on that."

She blinked up at me with those endlessly green eyes, and once again I wanted to fall into them. I was already leaning closer. So close I could almost kiss her…

"Wasn't that long ago you suggested I try it," she said. "Take the edge off, right? Escape reality. Be a little less uptight." She was teasing me, taunting me, but there was an edge to her words too. A baited hook.

"I was being a dick. I didn't mean it."

"No, you never do." She let out a deep sigh, her breath ghosting across my mouth.

I cupped her face. "I wouldn't wish it on my worst enemy, sparrow."

"I'm not your enemy. And lucky for both of us, I'm not your responsibility either." In a flash, she popped the pill and closed her mouth.

Fuck.

Images flashed behind my eyes—the poor souls in our facility, so strung out they could no longer tell whether they were dead or alive. All that mattered was the Black. The next hit. The comfortable numb.

Cold dread settled in my gut, and I squeezed her jaw. "Damn it, Haley. Spit it out."

She shook her head and pressed her lips into a tight line, the brat.

"Do *not* make me bite you," I warned. "And no, that's not the idle threat of a dick ex-boyfriend."

With a slow roll of her eyes, she finally did as I asked, and I plucked what was left of the pill from her tongue and set it on my own, for all the good it would do her. She'd never tried it before. It would take some time to kick in, but when it did, even that tiny little taste would fuck her up good.

Best I could hope for now was that she'd burn through the buzz quickly and pass out, then wake up tomorrow with a headache murderous enough to scare her away from the shit for good.

The headaches only happened your first time, but I wasn't about to tell her that. Better to let her believe the stuff was pure torture.

I closed my mouth and leaned back on the pillow, gazing up at the ceiling, but her soft touch on my cheek had me turning toward her again.

"I want to watch," she whispered. "Let me see it."

Powerless to refuse, I opened my mouth, frozen in place as her fingertips slid down along my jaw.

Haley was transfixed, mesmerized as the last of the pill dissolved, the magick swirling on my tongue and reflecting in her eyes.

"Do you feel it?" she asked.

I closed my mouth. Swallowed. "Not yet."

"Me neither. Maybe it's from an old batch."

"It's not an old batch, Haley. It's your first time—it might take a minute before you feel anything."

"What about you?"

I shook my head. "Half a pill? My body won't even register it."

"How many do you need before it registers?"

"Lately, three or four. I take what I can from the facility—whatever I think won't be missed."

The admission—both of them—burned on the way out, but if Haley was surprised or disappointed, she didn't say.

Instead, she closed her eyes and went quiet, and I did the same, and for a long time, neither of us moved.

She wasn't sleeping, though. Her heartbeat had quickened, her breathing jagged.

"What are you thinking about, little sparrow?" I finally asked, opening my eyes.

I found her already watching me.

Smiling, she said, "How did you know I wasn't sleeping?"

"I remember how you sound when you sleep, and this isn't it."

Her smile fell away and her eyes glazed with unshed tears.

"Tell me why you said his name," she whispered. "When the guards brought you to the throne room."

She was talking about Evander again, and this time, I couldn't keep it inside.

"Because when I looked into Keradoc's eyes, I thought I saw Evander's ghost." I sighed and shook my head. "I know how it sounds, Haley. The drugs talking, right? Or some trick of Keradoc's meant to confuse me. I *know* that now—so fucking obvious, right? But in that moment? I looked up into the face of the man who'd bested us, and I swore I saw... someone else."

"I... I saw someone else too, Elian. His face, his eyes... They kept changing. I thought... I thought he was you, and I—"

"*What*?" I sat up, my heart thudding in my chest.

"There's something I need to tell you. I don't know why I feel guilty... I mean, it's not like you and I are together, or... But I feel like you need to know, and it's..." She was babbling, talking a mile-a-minute, my heart jackhammering with every word, still hoping I hadn't heard her right, still hoping this story would end some other fucking way, and then...

"I kissed him, Elian," she said. "The night of the feast, when Keradoc first brought me to the throne room alone, I kissed him."

Fury burned through me. It was one thing to see her chatting him up in the library, offering him tea. It was one thing to see the way he looked at her.

But this?

Knowing she'd fucking *kissed* him?

"Why are you telling me this?" I ground out, practically throwing myself out of the bed.

"He was wearing your face!" she said, as if that explained it. She followed me out of bed, followed me right into the common room. "Your eyes!"

"You kissed a warlord because he glamoured himself to look like me? Is that supposed to—"

"Elian." She reached up and cupped my face, forcing me to look at her. "I kissed him because he *was* you. At least, that's what I believed. God, it was all so confusing. I hadn't seen you in days, and suddenly there you were. You—I mean, he—he'd taken me to the throne room. We were alone. I saw the glamour slip away, or—I don't know. Maybe he is Keradoc and your face was the glamour, but either way, in my mind, it was you."

I pulled out of her touch, turning my back on her. I couldn't look into those eyes right now, couldn't see the passion and longing in them, knowing that fae-fucking bastard had looked into those same eyes and seen those exact same things.

"Say something," she whispered. "Please."

"Fine. You want me to say something? Here it is, sparrow. I wish you'd never told me. I wish I didn't have to live the rest of my immortal life with that image stuck in my fucking brain. I wish..." I shoved my hands through my hair, ready to tear it all out. "Keradoc isn't just a warlord and a murderer, Haley. He's worse—so much worse."

"What are you talking about?" she asked. "What could be worse?"

"He's a trafficker, Haley. He steals fae kids from their home realms, enslaves them, and sells them off to his rich, noble friends. So yeah, you want to know what happened to Evander? Here's an idea—the next time you open your mouth for that fucking bastard Keradoc, why don't you ask *him* what happened instead of letting him stick his tongue down your throat."

I stormed out of that room, down the gallery hallway, down the stairs, and out into the dark streets of Amaranth City.

And there, in the loneliest fucking corner in the darkest, dankest alley I could find, I fell to my knees and screamed into the night until my throat bled and the ghosts in my heart fell still.

25

HALEY

My head clanged as if the bells of every cathedral in Italy had been relocated to the inside of my skull.

I wondered if Nona had something to do with it—a scolding from the great beyond. I smiled at the thought.

Last night, the Dream made me feel floaty and warm, but tonight there was only pain. Regret.

Still. Despite the ache in my body, I couldn't deny the appeal. I'd only gotten the barest taste of the stuff, yet when it finally kicked in, it sent me to another fucking planet.

Which was precisely why I wouldn't touch it again. It was too tempting. Too fucking dangerous.

"Sorry, am I interrupting?"

I glanced up at the now-familiar voice of Keradoc as he waltzed into the common room.

"Yes, but that's never stopped you before."

"No, I suppose it hasn't." He smiled, but tonight I found it irritating rather than charming. I was still feeling a bit prickly from the Dream, and at the sight of our warlord captor, all of Elian's warnings from last night came rushing back.

Keradoc isn't just a warlord and a murderer, Haley. He's worse—so much worse...

"Is there something you need, Keradoc?" I asked, my tone clipped. "Otherwise, I've got a lot of reading to do and a laundry list of missing ingredients to compensate for, so if you don't mind..."

"I need to go to the marketplace in East Amaranth," he said. "I thought—"

"Really? A whole castle full of servants, and suddenly you're doing your own shopping?" I narrowed my eyes. "Spill it. The truth, if you've got it. If not, kindly return later. I'm too tired right now to shovel bullshit."

He smiled again, and this time his cheeks flushed a bit. "Actually, my kitchen staff told me your gargoyle wasn't able to find all the ingredients you needed for your work. So I thought... I was wondering if you might... That is, if you're not too preoccupied with the spellwork... On second thought, forget I mentioned anything." He shook his head, flustered. "I'll... I'll leave you to it. Good evening, Haley."

I let out a deep sigh, still trying to reconcile everything in my mind.

The man Elian spoke of last night was a vicious criminal who deserved to be tortured, strung up by his balls, and dropped into his own moat for the most gruesome death possible. And everyone he'd ever wronged should be invited to piss on his corpse, and *then* he should be forced to come back as one of the ghouls, cursed for eternity.

But the man I looked at now? The man fumbling over his words to invite me for a stroll through the marketplace?

The man haunted by nightmares and ghosts?

The man who gave me visions of a dark, powerful future I hadn't stopped dreaming about?

The man who sometimes, when we first met, looked like Elian?

How could they be the same person?

Because you're fooling yourself on account of his epic dark-fae hotness, and every time he looks at you like that, you can't help but remember how good that kiss tasted...

No. That wasn't it. Not at all. I mean, sure. Obviously, I liked my men a little rough-around-the-edges, full of shadowy secrets and deep, dark wounds.

But I wasn't the fall-for-the-villain, blinded-by-Stockholm-Syndrome, he's-sexy-so-he-gets-a-pass-on-all-the-evil-doing type.

Still, something wasn't adding up. I had no idea who

our captor truly was, or what—if anything—he'd known about Evander's disappearance or the alleged kidnapping and trafficking of the other fae children Elian mentioned.

I didn't know who Evander was either, or anything about his true connection to Elian, who'd spoken about him as if he'd died long ago.

Maybe he had.

But deep down, my gut told me the man standing before me now wasn't behind any of it.

And the only way I was going to find out for sure was by spending more time with him.

Starting right now.

"Actually," I said, "I'd love to get out of the castle and pick up a few things. Just give me fifteen minutes to get changed."

A new smile broke across his face, making him look younger. Less troubled. "Great. Perfect. I mean, yes. Of course. I need to change as well. I'll meet you in the gallery."

I dressed quickly in some of the clothing he'd sent up for me, glad to finally have an excuse to wear it—black leather pants, a dark gray metallic shirt, platinum armlets, leather straps and belts for days. The whole thing was pretty badass.

Ready before Keradoc, I wandered down the gallery. The doors to his suite were ajar, and I couldn't help but sneak a quick peek inside.

The place was massive—probably three times the size of our entire suite, and that was just the part I could see. Everything was black—black walls, black furniture, black bedding.

And there, standing before a full-length mirror, was Keradoc. He'd just pulled on his shirt—but not before I saw the scars.

I held my breath to keep from gasping. His entire back and both arms were covered in scars—some thin and silver, others red and ropey. He'd been whipped, burned, shot, and the entire left side of his torso was mangled with some sort of vicious bite marks.

Heart in my throat, I stepped back from the doorway and scooted back to the stairwell, fighting to get my breathing under control.

When Jax and Elian had first told me about Keradoc, they'd said he wasn't even a real warlord. That he was a politician who played war games from behind a desk.

But if that were true, what the hell had happened to him?

And how the hell had he survived?

"Sorry to keep you," he said, and I glanced up, plastering on a smile. He looked over my outfit appreciatively, then pursed his lips. "Lovely, but I think it's missing something. Something to tie it all together."

Flashing one of his wicked grins, he handed over a bone-handled dagger.

My bone-handled dagger. The one Jax had given me that Keradoc had stolen the night of the feast.

"Seriously? You're trusting me with this?"

"It appears that I am. Don't make me regret it."

Before he could change his mind, I took it and fastened the sheath to one of my belts.

"Perfect," he said. "Besides, it's better to be safe than sorry in Amaranth City. My guards and I will be watching over you, of course, but… I'd just feel better knowing you had some way of defending yourself, should the need arise. Shall we?"

He held out his arm, and I linked mine through it, letting him escort me down the stairs.

Just before we headed outside, he said, "Oh, there's one more thing."

When I looked up, Keradoc was gone. The man who stood at my side now was blond, with striking amber eyes and a shorter, stockier build than the warlord's.

"Another glamour?" I asked.

"I can't risk being recognized in the marketplace. Not while I'm escorting you. I've got too many enemies, Haley. So as much as I despise wearing a glamour, I must remain incognito."

Two guards joined us outside—gargoyles in their human form—and together, we walked to the marketplace.

Before Keradoc had decided I was his secret weapon

and locked me up in the castle, I hadn't actually seen much of Amaranth City. Other than that first night in the pub with Gem, I'd spent most of my time in the apartment practicing my spells and going over our plans for the Feast of the Beast.

Since then, I'd seen the city only from a distance.

Now, up close and in the thick of it, I was experiencing massive sensory overload... And loving every minute of it.

The marketplace was packed with vendors selling goods out of stalls and carts—everything from weapons to spices to exotic meats to glittering jewelry. Crowds rolled through the narrow passageways like water, jostling each other to find the best bargains, haggling with the shop-keepers, stealing whatever they could get away with.

In less than an hour, I'd managed to find everything I needed, all paid for by Keradoc without question. He also bought me a hot cider and a pastry that reminded me of a giant Pop-Tart.

"So," I said, licking the last of the sugary, flaky crust from my fingertips. "At what point do you tell me this was all a setup and I'm actually about to meet my untimely demise?"

Keradoc laughed, low and smooth. "You still don't trust me, little thief?"

"You've spent the evening being nice to me and buying me things. I'd be a damn *fool* to trust you."

He laughed again, deeper this time, the skin around his

temporarily-amber eyes crinkling. They were the wrong color, but somehow I felt like I could still see the real Keradoc behind them.

I just didn't know who that real Keradoc was.

Still studying him, I recalled Elian's earlier accusations again, letting them roll around in my mind, trying to see if any of them stuck.

Murderer.

Kidnapper.

Fae child trafficker.

I knew the first was true—I'd seen him execute two shifters the night of the Feast. It was a thing I couldn't excuse, but... What if I didn't have the whole story? What if the shifters were guilty of crimes even more heinous than Keradoc's crime of beheading them?

And that night, Elian had mistaken Keradoc for Evander. He'd called him by that name several times. If Keradoc had been involved in Evander's death, wouldn't he have shown a glimmer of recognition? Guilt? Something?

I closed my eyes and shook my head. None of this made any sense.

"Haley? Are you all right?"

We'd stopped walking, I realized. I opened my eyes and forced a smile, intending to tell him I was fine.

But then, ducking into a building across the street, another fae caught my attention.

A Midnight fae with purple hair.

Everything inside me burned with rage.

"Gem," I hissed.

Keradoc turned to follow my line of sight.

When he looked at me again, he nodded. "Gem is supervising the operations your companions are working on. That's the processing and testing facility."

I handed over all my shopping bags. "Wait here," I said. "I'm going in."

"Not alone, you're not."

"Incognito, remember? You can't waltz in there with me and your goon squad. We'll draw too much attention."

"But—"

"No buts," I said. "You can wait for me right across the street. I just need five minutes. Ten tops."

Just enough time to bleed a bitch dry...

26

ELIAN

I'd been doing my level best to keep my shit together and do my job, but I'd also been high as *fuck* for the last two nights, so maybe I wasn't the best judge of my performance.

Gem had just returned from wherever the fuck she ran off to half the time, and as usual, she brought back a nasty glare for me. And a glower. And a roll of the eyes for good measure.

"How's it going?" she asked. I didn't know whether she was talking to me or Jax, but I decided to appoint myself spokesperson for that particular question.

"Excellent." I grinned, scooping up a handful of the little black beauties. "Truly excellent."

That, at least, was the truth.

This latest batch was our best yet—way more potent than the last, and it didn't wear off as quickly either. I had no doubts that any fae who tried it, Darkwinter or otherwise, would murder his own commander for a taste.

The high was fucking *exquisite*.

I thumbed at my chest and smiled again. "Exhibit A."

"Exhibit A, what?" she asked, and I realized I'd just said most of that shit inside my head.

Before I could repeat myself out loud, the front door banged open again, ushering in what I assumed was another desperate Amaranth City soul looking to volunteer as a test subject.

The woman was soft around the edges, a little smudgy. When I tried to focus on her, she doubled in my vision.

And both of them were marching toward us like they were on a *mission*.

"Haley?" I asked, finally recognizing her. She was just one person again, close enough to touch, so I reached out and fingered a lock of her hair. "Have you come to sing me to sleep, little sparrow?"

"Actually, I've come to stick a knife in *that* bitch's throat." She beelined right for Gem. Caught her off guard, too—enough to get that dagger pretty damn up-close-and-personal.

"Give me one reason not to slit your throat," she gritted out.

With another roll of her eyes, Gem arched a purple eyebrow, then touched Haley's shoulder.

That was it. One touch. One finger.

And Haley went down hard on her ass, her muscles spasming.

"Ouch," I said, remembering all too well the feeling of that zap.

Something deep inside me said I should probably be furious about what Gem had just done to Haley, but I couldn't seem to focus on that thought long enough to bring it to fruition.

Jax didn't seem to have any trouble with it, though. He was on Gem in a blink, grabbing a fistful of her shirt and hauling her close.

"Touch her again, *traitor*, and I don't care how many devil's trap bolts you threaten me with. I will *end* you."

"Yeah?" Gem laughed. "Let me know how that works out for you, cowboy."

And then she stalked off to harass someone else for a change, thank fuck.

"You'd think threatening the boss would get us canned," I said, finally realizing I should probably help Haley off the floor. She ignored my outstretched hand and got her own ass up, though.

Fine by me.

"Unfortunately for us," I continued, "we're too good at what we do. Job security, I guess." I popped another pill like it was fucking candy and grinned. "Boss says we're not supposed to steal from the stash, either. But I learned a little trick." I leaned in closed and fake-whispered in

Haley's ear, "It's not stealing if you say it's for quality control purposes."

"Control?" Haley snapped. "Interesting word choice for a man who's clearly *out* of control. Look around you, Elian. Is this what you want? Really?"

Her eyes flashed with anger, but there was sadness there too. Worry.

More shit I didn't need to see right now.

I shrugged as if I didn't give a fuck. Considering the amount of next-level Black I had coursing through my system, I shouldn't have been *capable* of giving a fuck, but still, there I was.

Giving fucks.

"No choice," I said, my words slurring. "You asked for my help getting to Midnight, and... Hell, sparrow. You were there every step of the way. You don't need me to give you the recap of how I landed *this* cushy job."

"I know you didn't have a choice with the job, Elian. I'm talking about..." She gestured behind me, a whole bunch of sympathy flooding her eyes now too. On top of everything else.

I didn't need to turn around to know she was talking about the Dreamers.

My fucking people, for all intents and purposes.

"So you've gone from dancing with the Devil to turning your nose up at it in a matter of..." I glanced at my wrist as if I were wearing a watch. "Ten hours? Might be a new flip-flop record for that not-so-shiny moral compass of yours, Haley."

Her eyes blazed, and she opened her mouth like she was about to spit venom. Or fire. Or venomous fire, all of which I'd welcome.

Because in that moment?

Yeah, I wanted the fight. Needed it. Needed her to hurl those insults my way, sharp daggers I could catch right in the heart.

Anything—*anything* to feel something other than this soul-sucking void chewing through me.

But my little sparrow wouldn't give me that. She was too good for it. Yeah, she was pissed, but that was only because she was so damn worried.

I knew her well enough to know she wasn't truly judging me. Wasn't judging those poor souls lined up behind me with their mouths open for the next pill, their eyes rolled back, their bodies quaking, some of them so far gone they didn't even realize they were sitting in their own waste.

"Why?" she whispered, her voice breaking. "Why do you do it?"

"Because sometimes there's a hole inside that's so fucking big, nothing can fill it. And sometimes there's a *lot* of holes—gaping fucking craters—and in case you haven't figured it out yet, sparrow, that's where I'm at. Gaping fucking craters."

"And this?" she asked softly, plucking a pill from the pile in my hand and rolling it across her palm. "This can fill them?"

"No." This time, she didn't fight me when I tried to take it from her. Just let me have it, watched as I tossed it into my mouth. "All it does is make me high enough to numb the edges a little. But I'll take being high and numb over the full-blown pain of my reality any day."

"Even if that reality includes people who care about you? People who... people who love you?"

"People who love me? Please. Even *I* couldn't conjure up a fantasy *that* good."

Hurt flooded her eyes, and I knew at once I'd said the wrong thing again.

Earlier tonight, Jax had told me I was poison to her, and that motherfucker was right. Every time I looked at her, every time I opened my mouth, all the wrong words fell out.

Because I wasn't allowed to say the right ones.

I wasn't trying to hurt her. But then, neither was a poison trying to kill its victim. That was just its nature.

Now, once again, I struggled to find the words to fix the mess I'd made, to explain how I didn't mean half the dumb shit I said, to string something together that made a fucking *lick* of sense amidst all the bullshit.

But Haley was already heading for the door, Jax

following after her, two of the only three people I cared about leaving me to fall back into those dark craters alone.

So I did what I do best.

Popped another pill, sat down with the other dreamers, and waited to catch the next wave to fucking oblivion.

27

HALEY

I hadn't realized I was running until I felt Jax's hands on my shoulders from behind, slowing me to a stop not far from the nameless tavern where we'd met up with Gem my first night here.

The sight of it—the reminder of what she'd done to us, the reminder of her smug face inside that awful facility—only fueled my anger. If not for her, would we have been back in New Orleans by now? Would I have gotten Keradoc's blood and satisfied Melantha's demands? Would my sisters be free from her ever-present threat?

Would Elian have already turned his back on the drug that had so thoroughly imprisoned him?

"Let me go." I tried to shrug off Jax's touch, but it was a weak effort, and we both knew it.

Gently, he turned me around to face him.

"Tell me what's going on," he said softly. "Let me see what's behind those eyes."

I looked up, unable to stop the tears from spilling.

"I'm sorry we didn't tell you about Gem," he said. "Keradoc assigned her to supervise. Saint and I didn't want you to worry."

"It's not just Gem, as much as I want to stab her with something rusty." I shook my head. "I hate seeing him like that, Jax. It breaks my heart."

"I know, angel. I know." He drew me in close, his warm embrace and campfire-and-lemons scent grounding me. "You shouldn't have seen it. Any of it. Keradoc never should've brought you here."

I pulled back and smeared away the tears. "But even if I *hadn't* seen it, it's still happening to him. He's still going through it and I'm just... God, I feel so helpless."

"Saint's problems are not your burdens to bear. Believe me, I've tried, and that's the fastest way to an early grave."

"But he's my—"

"Your what, Haley?" He sighed and released me, suddenly defensive. "Your ex? Your first love? Your *only* love?"

I searched his face, trying to get a read on his emotions. He knew how I felt about Elian, and he'd never gotten worked up about it before. Not like this. So no, it wasn't jealousy tightening his voice, despite how badly he wanted me to believe it.

It was pain. Anguish.

I knew in my bones Jax cared deeply for Elian, despite everything they'd been through. Maybe even because of it. They were truly brothers, in all the ways that counted.

And I knew this was killing him as much as it was killing me.

"No, Jax," I said softly. "I was going to say family. Elian is my family. And no, it's not perfect. It's messy and complicated and crazy and *hard*. So much harder than it should be. All I know is I feel like we're watching him kill himself, one little pill at a time, and there's not a damn thing I can do about it."

Jax scoffed and shook his head. "Whatever."

His flippancy ignited my rage all over again. "Fine. You look at him, and all you see is a fuckup—I get it. I see his mistakes too, Jax. So many of them. Hell, that man is a walking reminder of the darkest nights of my life. But I still care about him. I don't want him to..." I trailed off, unable to say the words.

Die.

Take his own life.

Overdose.

Succumb.

Fall.

"You think I want Saint to kill himself, Haley?" he spat. "You think I want to stand by and watch him disappear, or worse—turn into one of those strung-out corpses back there? A hollowed-out shell of a person? They're barely breathing, for fuck's sake!"

"Yeah? And how much easier would your life be if Elian suffered the same fate?"

"*Way* easier—no question. But easier doesn't… Damn it, Haley. It doesn't mean better." Then, softer than the breeze down the rancid alley, he whispered, "My heart is broken too, angel. And every night I see him like this, every night I have to decide whether to watch him suffer through withdrawals or give him another pill to take away his pain, it breaks my heart a little more."

A tear slipped down his cheek, and he brushed it away.

"Then why do you do it?" I asked. "Why do you do it at all? In all the years you two have been stuck together, why the hell haven't you left him? And don't tell me it's because of some weird demonic principles about carrying debts and who owes who. It's more than that and you know it."

"I've told him a thousand times I'm going to leave. Hell, before we left New Orleans, I swore to him if we made it out of Midnight alive a second time, I was packing my shit and leaving for good. But that was all bullshit. I stay because he needs me. I stay because when I needed him, he was there. Maybe not in the way I wanted him to be, but still. He was there. So yeah, maybe it *would* be easier if he just fucked off and died, sparing us all the torture of watching this shit. Of cleaning up his messes. But when you call someone a brother—when you make that oath—

it's not just for the perfect, squeaky clean stuff, Haley. It's just like you said—messy and complicated and hard. That's what you sign up for when you choose your family, and as much as it fucks me up inside, no, I *wouldn't* have it any other way. You ask me why I stay? I stay because I *choose* to. Every day, every moment, that choice presents itself again—stay or go. And I make it. I stay. I will *always* stay. With Saint. With Hudson. With you, because you're my fucking family. So if you can't trust that—if after all this time you actually think I'm the kind of guy who walks out when shit gets real—then maybe you're not the woman I thought you were."

"Jax, that's not—"

"Haley, there you are." Keradoc appeared around the corner, trailed by his two guards. "I was worried you'd finally run off."

Jax glared at me, as if he were waiting for me to tell Keradoc to go fuck himself.

When I didn't, he just shook his head and scoffed like he couldn't believe he'd wasted so many weeks of his life with me.

Then, without another word, he turned on his heel and stormed off toward the facility, knocking into Keradoc's shoulder as he passed.

Keradoc let it go, his eyes never leaving mine. "Are you all right?"

"I'm fine. Just... just take me—" I caught myself before I

said the word balanced on the tip of my tongue. *Home.* "Take me back to the castle. Please, Keradoc. I just need to be alone right now."

28

HUDSON

I'd never been big on cultural shit like the ballet or the opera or all them gallery tours. Back in New Orleans, that'd always been Saint's bag. My boy liked to take his rich vampire clients out for a show—all part of the fake-ass fantasy that scoring a bunch of Black from a fae dealer was a classy affair, not some shady back-alley drug trade.

Who the fuck had time to wade through that much bullshit? To sit through some boring-ass, artsy-fartsy show, oohing and ahhing and jerking off about metaphors and color palates and artistic integrity just to seal a deal both parties knew was a sure thing anyway?

I never understood it.

But now, watching Haley work her magick?

God *damn*, that felt like watching a fine artist carve a

statue out of marble or paint the ceiling of some sacred place, her every move a study in elegance and grace, her eyes dancing with a passionate light that warmed every part of me.

She was a work of art. A gift from the gods the rest of us had no business even looking at, yet there I was, lurking in the shadows in a state of awe and wonder as she brought her blood magick to life.

I'd just flown back after wrapping up Keradoc's latest assignment—helping his guards secure a newly discovered field of corpsevine just north of the Boiling Glass Sands—when I noticed the tell-tale red glow shining from our balcony. I knew I should've left her in peace, let her practice her spells alone, but I couldn't help myself.

Now, I stayed hidden behind a pillar of obsidian while she kneeled in a pentacle made of dirt and muttered her latest spell, two bowls of blood on the ground before her, both glowing red.

When she finished her spell, the bowls glowed brighter, but then fizzled out quickly.

"No," she hissed. "No no no... *Damn* it! Why? Why have you forsaken me? Have *thou* forsaken? Hast thou? Ugh." She tilted her face to the moons and shook her fist.

I couldn't help the laugh that slipped out. She was so fucking cute.

She heard me though. Let out a little yelp and jumped back, hand pressed to her heart.

Busted, I stepped out of the shadows and shrugged, like, *what are ya gonna do?*

"Didn't see you there, Gargs." Her eyes widened as she took in the sight of me, then my girl cracked up. She swept a hand up and down, indicating my naked form. "Wow, so you're pretty much always free-balling it these days, huh?"

"What can I say? I like the feel of the wind on my—"

"Biceps. I get it."

I laughed again—couldn't be helped. Hell, the woman had made me smile more in a few weeks than anyone else had in my entire existence. "Gargoyles ain't got the same hangups about flesh that you humans do. Not that I don't appreciate and venerate certain forms of it, mind you. Just that I don't feel a sudden need to duck and cover after I shift back into human form."

"Nor should you." She crossed the balcony to meet me in the middle and grinned up at me, stretching up to loop her arms around my neck, seemingly undisturbed by my nudity.

"Careful," I teased. "Keep greeting me like this after a hard night's work, and I might start getting used to it."

"Like I'm getting used to seeing your naked, tattooed ass on full display?"

"No one said you had to look."

"As if I could tear my gaze away." She let out a dreamy sigh. "Maybe you're onto something though. Maybe *I* should try it. Saunter around the castle in the nude. Give

Keradoc's guards something to gossip about besides the size of their swords."

"Hate to rain on your parade, but that's *definitely* not happening. Long as those creeps are near, you're staying fully clothed. Matter fact, why aren't you wearing a coat? And a scarf? And maybe a cape, just to cover the bases?"

"Excuse me?" she teased. "That's hardly fair."

"Just saving lives, babygirl." I picked her right up, tucking her close against my chest as I carried her to the far edge of the balcony. "Anyone other than my boys so much as twitched an *eyelid* near your fine naked self, I'd snap their heads off, dump out the shit-for-brains inside, and use their empty skulls as beer mugs and no, I wouldn't feel bad about it. Not even a little."

Haley laughed. "That was... oddly specific. Very creepy. But also kind of sweet? In your own special gargoyle way, I suppose."

"As it was meant," I said with a wink that had her shaking her head and laughing. I set her on a flat part of the barrier and took a seat next to her. "Speaking of shit-for-brains... Where are the boys? They usually beat me back home."

Her eyes dimmed, the smile dropping from her face. With a deep sigh, she said, "As far as I know, they're still at the facility. I haven't seen them at all these last two nights. I'm pretty sure they're avoiding me."

"What? Why?"

"Keradoc took me to the market. I saw the facility. Things got... heated."

She told me the story—all the crazy shit she'd seen, the bullshit with Gem, her fears about Saint, her fight with Jax.

"I'm so worried about them, Gargs," she said softly. "And when I saw all that, it just hit me really hard, and I just opened my big, fat mouth and stepped *right* in it. I tried to wait up for them last night so I could smooth things over, but I passed out before they got back. I wouldn't be surprised if they decided to stop talking to me altogether."

"No. No fuckin' way."

I saw the way they looked at her—Jax like he was always ready to step in front of a flaming arrow to keep her safe, Saint like he wanted to turn himself inside out just to erase the sadness from her eyes.

Sadness I was pretty damn sure he'd put there in the first place.

So what, they'd argued. Didn't make a damn bit of difference. Nothing she could do or say would send either one of them packing, and I told her as much.

"I hope you're right." She curled up against my chest, and I tucked her in close, just holding her. Breathing her in.

We sat like that for a long time, me and Haley.

Silence had never been a problem for us. Lots of people thought silence was awkward—they couldn't deal with it. But with Haley, it'd always felt like a respite—a little place we could retreat to together and just... just breathe.

Just be.

After a while, she pulled back and smiled up at me again. "I'm glad you stopped by. I needed a break from all this summoning business."

"Yeah. I suppose I should leave you to it." I stood up, and she followed, already shaking her head.

"Confession? I don't want you to leave."

"Confession?" I blew out a relieved sigh. "I wasn't planning to leave. I was just gonna go sit in the dark where you couldn't see me and keep right on watching anyway."

"Seriously?"

"Couldn't leave you if I tried, babygirl. Not really."

"Can I tell you something crazy? I mean, you're used to that from me, right?"

I grinned and took her hand. Brought it to my mouth and kissed her palm. "Lay it on me."

"When I'm with you, I feel this... this intense connection. It started that first day in the garden at Elian's place, even before I'd met you. When I touched you? There was this weird spark and I *swore* you felt it too. Even through the stone."

I squeezed her hand and nodded. "I thought I was going crazy too. But that wasn't it. We do have a connection, Haley. Runs deep."

"I feel connected to all of you. Elian and I... well, we have history, obviously. Jax came out of nowhere, but my feelings for him came on fast and furious. And you... I can't even explain it. I just know that when I'm with you, I feel like nothing bad could ever touch me."

"None of that sounds crazy to me."

"There's more. It's... it's this whole place, Hudson." She looked out across the city and sighed. "I feel connected to Midnight too. The magick, the air, the stones, the stars and moons. God, even Keradoc is—well, I won't say I've got any love for the creep. But I'm starting to understand him a little. I don't think he's evil, Gargs. A complete douche, yes. But not an *evil* douche, which feels like an important distinction. Anyway, the longer I'm here, the more I feel like I was always supposed to end up here. Like maybe I just got lucky all these years—somehow, I stayed off the radar, and the Midnight fae never came looking for me."

When she looked up at me again, her eyes were glassy, and I swore I saw all the red-and-gold stars in the sky reflecting right back at me.

"Do you remember the roses?" she asked.

"Beauty in the darkness, babygirl."

She nodded and held out her hands, studying her

palms like she was trying to memorize every line etched in them.

When she finally spoke again, I had to dip my head low just to catch her whisper.

"Do you think I'm evil, Hudson? Like the Darkwinter fae?"

My heart cracked in half at the pain in her eyes.

"Evil isn't a bloodline, Haley. It's a choice we make. Don't always feel that way for some, I suppose, but it's still a choice. Darkwinter fae... Hell, they're just trying to make their way in this world, protect what's theirs. Same as Keradoc. Same as you and me."

"Yeah, but the things they have to do to protect what's theirs? To save the people or places they love? Maybe that's where the evil comes in."

"Does it?" I ran a hand across my beard and shrugged. "Then sign me up for team evil, because I'm telling you *right* now. Anyone comes out here—soldier, gargoyle, Keradoc himself—and threatens your life? I'm taking that fucker down. I will *not* hesitate." I tucked a finger under her chin and tilted her face up, waiting for her to meet my eyes again. "No one with love in their heart is evil, babygirl. But all of us are capable of doing evil shit. Beyond that, I can't make a blanket call. None of us can."

"So you're saying there's a chance I'm evil?"

"I'm saying it's a word, a label. And it's not up to you to decide—it'll be written by your enemies, if it's written at all. But if you really wanna know? No, babygirl. I don't think you're evil. Far as I'm concerned, you're just... well, you're the right amount of bad."

She laughed and wiped away a tear. "I guess I can live with that."

A cool breeze skated on through, making her shiver. I flexed my shoulders and let my wings unfurl, curling one around her to block the wind.

"You can do that?" she gasped. "Wings, even when you're totally in human form?"

"It's a partial shift, yeah. Not that great for actual flying —the human body isn't made for it. Mostly I just use it to impress the ladies."

"Well, it's working."

I laughed, but soon it faded away, the serious shit rising back up to the surface.

I had to tell her.

Now or never.

"Haley, there's something I need you to know. That connection you feel? You're right. I feel it too. From the first time I saw you walk into Saints and Sinners, and no, it wasn't just 'cause of that hot little dress you had on."

"It *was* a hot dress though, wasn't it?"

I nodded, but I couldn't stop to joke. This was too important. I had to get it out before I ran out of words.

"Gargoyles... We have mate bonds. And for whatever reason, the universe—or fate, or the stars, or whatever you want to call it? Something saw fit to make you mine. Mine to protect and guard. Mine to cherish. Mine to love. That don't mean we have to... you know. Be *in* love. But there's the potential. Either way, the bond will tie us for life."

"Mate bonds?" She looked up at me, her eyes wide, a smile tugging at her lips. "I'm your mate? As in, fated mate?"

"That's one way to put it, yeah."

"Is that how you were able to sense I was in trouble the night of the feast?"

"Sure was. And I suspect that's how I got out of that cave, too. Your fear... I felt it through the bond. It just... it fucking *enraged* me, babygirl. So one minute I was locked in stone, and the next thing I knew, I felt you—felt that panic. Something just exploded inside me, and suddenly the spell they'd used on me shattered. I shifted into my warrior form, ready to murder some motherfucker just to find my way back to you. And that's just what I did."

She held my gaze for so long, not saying a word, I thought maybe she was about to laugh. Or worse—cry. Or, worse yet, run back into the suite and lock my ass out here.

But then she just smiled up at me with her sweet Haley-smile, and said the one thing I didn't even realize I needed to hear.

"Well, that's fucking cool."

Now, I laughed. "Cool? I tell you we have this mystical

fated connection that may or may not lead to love, and you go with 'cool?' No questions, no denials, nothing?"

She shook her head, her face turning serious. "No, Gargs. I can't explain it, but it just... I don't know. It just feels right. Like, as soon as you said it, something clicked in my mind, and I thought, of *course* we're fated mates."

"In that case, I need to ask you something, babygirl, and I need you to be real straight with me."

"Always," she whispered.

"The way I see it, you got a choice to make. And whatever you pick, I'm good with it—no questions asked, no pressure, no awkwardness between us. That night when I told you I got you? There's no expiration date on that. I'm here for you no matter what. *That* is a promise."

She nodded. "And it means more to me than you know."

"Here it is, then." I blew out a breath. Jumped in headfirst, no net, hoping like hell I wouldn't crash and burn. "You're either gonna ask me to kiss you right now, or you're gonna send me to bed with a broken heart. Pick one."

I smiled to let her know I was kidding—sort of. But she just... well god *damn*, her whole face lit up like I'd just told her I found a way to bust us all out of here.

"That's it?" she asked. "Just two choices? No third option, no clauses or sub-clauses, no contingencies?"

"Just the two. So what'll it be, beautiful?"

"Hmm." She smirked. "I may be bad, Gargs, but

sending some poor, defenseless gargoyle home with a broken heart? *That* would make me downright terrible."

"Agreed."

"And I'm not terrible."

"Not in the slightest."

"I think I'm more—"

"Haley? I love hearing you ramble. I swear it. But right now, I *really* need to kiss you. So if you could make your decision and put me outta my misery, I'd appreciate it."

"I *really* need you to kiss me, so that works out well. And also—"

I didn't get to know what she was planning to say after that. Swallowed up her damn words with a kiss so deep, so devastating I thought maybe we created a whole new galaxy with the explosion.

The bond, fate, the stars, destiny, whatever the fuck you wanted to call it...

That shit had *nothing* on this.

Yeah, she was mine to protect. Mine to watch over. But what I felt right now as she slid her arms around me, as she parted her mouth, as I deepened that kiss and unleashed a sweet little moan from between her cherry-red lips?

That was more than the bond.

That was love, or a good deal of the way to it.

When we finally broke for air, we were both a little bewildered. Took us a minute to realize we'd accidentally knocked over one of the bowls of blood. It mixed with the Midnight dirt, glowing brightly.

"Hudson, look," she gasped.

And there on the ground between us, a whole 'nother mess of them black roses of hers bloomed in the moonlight.

29

HUDSON

"Hudson?" She glanced at the flowers, then back up at me, her eyes filled with a mix of wonder and fear. "I know you said there's beauty in darkness, but this whole black-roses thing is seriously starting to freak me out."

I stared down into her pretty face, her sparkling eyes. My lips still tingled from her kiss. Hell, she was honey and spun sugar and all the brightest stars in the blackest sky.

But she was my spooky little monster girl too, and right now, I needed her to know just how much I appreciated it—all of it.

"Haley," I growled, determined to make her listen. To make her believe it. "I've never seen anything so fucking remarkable as you and your black-magick roses. So whatever worries you got about that? Squash it, babygirl. You've got nothing to be ashamed of."

"Do you mean it?" she whispered, the sweetest little smile curving her mouth.

"Wouldn't say it if I didn't. Figured you knew that about me by now."

"Hmm. Maybe I just like hearing you talk."

"That so?" I pulled her close to me again, running my nose down along hers and dusting her lips with another kiss. Damn, one kiss and I was already addicted to her. "What else you like?"

My wings hovered over us, fluttering in the breeze, and she glanced up at them and smiled even bigger. "I like the wings, Gargs. A lot."

I stretched them out, giving her a show.

"Can I touch them?" she asked. "Or is that... not a thing you're supposed to ask? I'm sorry. You're my first gargoyle."

"And you're my first little monster girl," I said with a wink, "so I guess I'll allow it."

I kissed her forehead, tucked my wings in close, then turned and got down on my knees, giving her unrestricted access.

She ran her fingertips along the edges, then flattened her hands, stroking me with her palms.

I shuddered in the wake of her touch.

"What does it feel like when I touch you?" she asked.

"It feels..." My words trailed off into a groan of pleasure. "God *damn*. Do that again."

With a soft laugh that whispered across my skin, she

stroked the edge of one wing, then the other, back and forth with the gentle touch of her fingertips, then the soft scrape of her nails, her every movement driving me wild.

I had no idea how long she stood there mapping my skin with her fingers, but it felt like hours. Hours and hours of sheer bliss as I lost myself to her sweet caress, every stroke sizzling with the magick of our bond.

By the time she came around and knelt down in front of me, I was so hard for her it hurt, no way to hide it. She continued her soft strokes, grazing my chest, my abs, lower, fucking *lower*, until my little monster girl finally wrapped those fingers around my cock.

I hissed through my teeth. Fucking hell, her touch was like living fire. It'd been so long since anyone had touched me—centuries. And Haley? She was in a league of her own. Just being near her made it hard to breathe. Now she had her hand on my cock, her wet mouth parted, her eyes blazing with a fire that seemed to be *daring* me to cross that final line with her...

How had I not dropped dead of a fucking heart attack yet?

How had Jax and Saint survived her?

"Hudson," she whispered, her voice turning shy, that fire in her eyes dimming a little, though she didn't let go of my cock—a thing I was *supremely* grateful for. "Is this really happening?"

Everything was so oversensitive, so hot for her, all my

wires felt like they were short-circuiting. I could *think* the words, but couldn't seem to make my lips move.

Once again, I'd forgotten how to fucking talk. But this time it wasn't because of some unspeakable trauma.

It was because she'd left me tongue-tied, my nerves buzzing, my muscles trembling for more.

Damn it. Much as I loved the feel of her touch on my wings, I needed to be a man for this. *All* man, or I wouldn't be able to concentrate long enough to find those words I so badly needed to find.

I flexed my shoulders and shifted the rest of the way into my human form, no trace of the warrior left, other than the heart jackhammering inside my chest. A warrior's heart that'd somehow never beat as hard in battle as it was beating right now, all for this woman. This witch. My mate.

"I'm... sorry," she whispered as my wings vanished, confusion smothering the last of the fire in her eyes. "Did I... did I hurt you? I thought... Maybe I was too rough? I wasn't sure if—"

I pressed my fingertips to her lips and shook my head. It was all I could manage in the moment, but I needed her to know it was okay. More than okay.

She smiled softly, and I knew she understood me, just like always.

"I'll give you a minute to find the words," she said. "But I've got some for you first, if you don't mind?"

I nodded. I loved her words. All of them. Always.

"I need you to know something too," she said. "I believe you about the bond—I feel it too, and it means more to me than I could ever say, which sounds crazy since I never seem to run out of things to say. But I'm doing this because I want to, Hudson. I want *you*. Not just as a friend and protector and a fated mate, or whatever you call it. But something more."

She stood and stripped out of her clothes, revealing herself to me in the moonlight, naked and perfect and damn near stealing my breath away.

I held her at arm's length, searching her face, unable to hide my goofy grin.

I wanted something more too. All of it.

"But if that's not where you intended things to go tonight," she continued, "then you can be honest with me about that. Words, notes, hand gestures—however you need to say it, just say it. No games, no sugar coating. Not with us."

The fire in her eyes, in her voice... It finally broke through the haze in my mind.

I fisted her hair and brought her close, running my nose along her jaw, inhaling her scent. Desire rumbled up through my chest, my throat tight with it. "Haley fucking Barnes. How can you not know?"

"I know it seems obvious, right? I mean, all the signals are there." She glanced down at my hard length and smiled. "But I can't make guesses and assumptions. Not with this—it's too important to me. *You're* too important. So please, Hudson. Tell me what you want."

"You need to hear me say it, then?"

She bit her plump lower lip. Nodded. That sweet blush darkened her cheeks, and I could tell from the tightness in her shoulders she was holding her breath.

Time to end this torture... for both of us.

"What I *want*," I growled, "is for you to ride my face until *you're* trembling and *I* can't remember the taste of any damn thing in the world but you. I don't need notes, don't need hand gestures, and I sure as shit don't intend to play games. I just need you in my mouth so I can make you come so hard you forget how to fucking *breathe*. That clear enough for you?"

She gasped, her cheeks blushing a few shades deeper, and for a second I wondered if I'd pushed it too far.

But then my girl just busted up laughing, a sound that made my heart kick up a few more gears.

"Oh, you think that's funny, do you?" I teased. "I'll give you funny." I grabbed her in a bear hug and dropped, taking her right down with me. I stretched out flat on my back in her bed of black roses and dirt, Haley straddling me, heat radiating from every inch of her.

"Seriously?" She was still laughing. "*Seriously?*"

"Depends on what you're seriously-ing me about."

"Before tonight, I could've counted the number of

words you've said out loud on one hand. Maybe two. Now you're coming at me with words like *that*?"

"Yeah, well. Ain't no point in mincing them now, right?"

She leaned forward, hands sliding up over the tattoos covering my pecs, her hair falling against my face. Her mouth was kissably close when she whispered, "Say more, Hudson."

The taste of my name on her breath... *Fuck*.

I swept back her hair, gathering it in my fist at the base of her neck so I could see her eyes. They glittered like emeralds in the darkness, two bright jewels that felt like another gift from the gods.

"I loved kissing your sweet mouth," I said softly, "But now it ain't enough. I need to kiss you *everywhere*, Haley. I need to know just what my spooky little monster tastes like as I make her shatter."

"Holy shit," she breathed. "Where have *you* been hiding, filthy-mouthed gargoyle superhottie?"

"I'm not hiding, babygirl. I'm right here. And I need *you* to get your fine ass right up—" I grabbed her hips and hauled her close until she was finally straddling my face. "*—here*."

Another gasp slipped out from her cherry-red mouth, her thighs brushing against my ears as she hovered above me, still just out of reach.

I slid my hands up and cupped her ass, urging her

closer, a groan of frustration rumbling through my chest. "Closer."

"So impatient," she teased. "Naughty gargoyle."

"You're killing me." *Fuck.* At that point, I was pretty sure I'd turn to stone and crumble into dust if she refused me for even one more minute. "No more talking. *Please*, baby-girl. Let me taste you."

The desperation in my voice was pathetic, but that shit was real. I felt it all the way down to my bones, that deep ache for her, the feeling that she belonged to me in ways that went beyond the mate bond. Ways I wanted to show her right the hell *now*.

A soft breeze whispered across the balcony, making her shiver. Her nipples hardened, and she leaned her head back and let out a sigh of pleasure.

And finally—fucking *finally*—Haley lowered herself down, her hands fisting my hair, holding on for the ride.

My mouth was on her in a heartbeat, stealing the taste I'd wanted for so long, licking and teasing and kissing her and… fuck *me*. She started moving, rocking her hips—slow at first, then grinding down against me as she lost herself in the pleasure.

Pleasure I was more than happy to give her.

I was so turned on, all I wanted to do was grab my cock, stroke, and fall right over the edge with her. But that would mean taking my hands off her ass, and some motherfuck-er'd have to chop off my arms before *that* would happen.

So I ignored the ache in my stone-hard cock and focused entirely on her, on making her squirm, on making her gasp as I licked and sucked and devoured her until I finally got my wish.

There was no other taste in the world but her.

And when that sweet little tremble I so desperately wanted to feel finally rippled through her thighs... When she tossed her head back and gasped my name over and over as she came all over my face...

Hell, if I wasn't already halfway in love with her before?

That did it. That fucking did it.

30

HALEY

I'd always wanted to be ravaged.

And as it turned out, my sweet teddy bear—my fated mate—was a ravager.

The sounds of his deep, gravelly moans vibrated through me, his beard tickling my thighs, his demanding mouth so fucking amazing...

God, I wanted it to last all night.

But Hudson was too good, his kisses too intense, and it wasn't long before the first ripples of pleasure were already rolling through me.

When I finally came, I gasped, calling out his name, tears flooding my eyes, my heart thundering until slowly, beat by beat, it settled back down.

I pulled back, lying down to curl up beside him.

When he met my gaze again, his eyes were dazed, his mouth curved in a sweet and sexy grin.

"You gave me what I want," he said softly. "Now tell me what *you* want, babygirl."

"As if that wasn't enough?"

"Apparently, it wasn't." He ran a thumb along my lower lip, shaking his head with a mock frown. "I don't hear you singing."

"Give a witch a minute, Gargs!" I laughed, everything in me buzzing and light. "I'm still trying to catch my breath!"

"Don't bother. I'm only going to steal it again." He captured my mouth in another kiss, his beard still damp with the evidence of what he'd done to me, and the thought of him wearing my scent like that...

It sent another jolt of pleasure right through my core.

I wanted him inside me.

Now.

I pulled back. Grinned up at him. "So, about those wings..."

"You want the wings?" He flipped us so he was on top, then flexed his shoulders, and his wings unfurled once more, curling around us and cocooning us in our own dark little world.

I reached up and ran my fingertips along the inside edges, making him shiver.

"You have *no* idea what that does to me," he growled.

"Is it like that with everything that touches you? The breeze? Another person?"

"Breeze feels nice, sure. But it ain't got shit on you,

Haley. It's you. Your touch, your... your everything. I can't explain it."

"Does it—"

The sound of another pair of wings fluttering—not Hudson's—cut off my words.

I lifted my head with a start, shocked to find one of Keradoc's gargoyles standing on the balcony and glaring down at us, supremely annoyed.

And I was pretty sure he was one of the assholes who'd shot magickal arrows at us the night Hudson had pulled me out of the Sanctuary.

Before I could even grab my clothes and cover up, Hudson had already gotten to his feet and shifted into his warrior form. His wings blocked me from view, and I stood up and tugged on my clothes, more than ready to push this asshole off the balcony.

"Stay behind me, babygirl," Hudson whispered. His voice was soft, but the warning in his tone sent a chill skittering down my spine.

The other gargoyle lifted his hands, as if to show he meant no harm. "Relax. I'm here on official Midnight business."

"Tell Keradoc I'm busy," I snapped. *Shit.* Things were just getting good out here, too. Well, good *again*.

"Keradoc is in a meeting with his generals," he said. "I'm here at the behest of Gem."

"Gem?" I laughed, shifting to stand in front of Hudson.

"You can tell *her* to fuck right off the edge of—"

"It's the vampire-fae, Miss Barnes. There's been an incident at the facility. He's... not well."

Alarm shot through my veins. "Elian? What happened?"

"I don't know the details. I was asked to find you and bring you back."

"Gem?" I asked. "Gem asked you to find me?"

"Gem and the one-eyed demon both. The demon told me I'd likely have trouble convincing you it was a legitimate request, so he sent a message. Something about the saint needing his little sparrow, and it's time to make the choice—stay or go. I assume you know what that means?"

I looked at Hudson, and my gargoyle mate nodded, no questions asked. No debate.

"It means," I said to the guard as Hudson scooped me into his arms, "we're going. Step aside—I've got my own ride."

31

KERADOC

Weeks ago, I demanded regular reports from the Road of Silence. And in all that time, my highest-ranking officers have provided little more than shrugs and guesswork." I tossed the papers across the table, shaking my head.

More reports. More bullshit. More empty words that would never help us win this war.

"It appears the Darkwinter fae are lying low, sir," the general said.

"It *appears*? Or it is *fact*? Only one of those things is even remotely useful to me. Care to guess which one?"

"Facts, sir."

"Yes. Facts. So if you do not have facts to provide, then *you* are not useful to me either. Dismissed."

"But sir, we must—"

"Dismissed!" I shouted.

The general rose from his chair as ordered, but his face looked stricken.

Once, they'd been used to my short temper, my gruff demeanor.

My cruelty.

I'd let it fade in recent months. Gone too easy on them.

Mistake.

One of them—the general overseeing the southern outpost—hadn't even shown up tonight.

They were losing respect for me. Growing complacent.

But as much as I'd love to blame the incompetence of my generals for my current mood, I couldn't. The foulness that had crept into my bones tonight was all on account of one infuriating, passionate, beautiful, untouchable blood witch.

I scarcely remembered having a life before Midnight, though I knew from my nightmares I hadn't always lived here. Still, I'd gotten so accustomed to this realm, I hardly noticed its charms anymore. Not just the magick humming through the rocks or the splendor of the triple moons, but the small things that made a city unique in *every* realm—the food, the people, the sights and the scents, the oddities.

Showing her around Amaranth City, I saw everything through new eyes. Through *her* eyes.

She'd moaned in pleasure at the taste of our food, our cider. She stared in wide-eyed wonder at the crowded marketplace, her eyes darting from one vendor to the next, excitement coloring her cheeks. She'd laughed for me, and her smile had felt like the sun upon my face—a sun I only ever saw in my dreams.

Yet that smile was fleeting. It had never been meant for me.

Only for them. Her demon. Her vampire-fae. The gargoyle I'd watched pleasuring her on the balcony tonight, making her smile in ways I could only dream of.

They were the monsters who held her heart.

Me? I was nothing more than a merchant. The bastard warlord she'd bargained with for a fair trade—the safety of her sisters and companions in exchange for the ritual that would bring me the so-called weapon to destroy my enemies.

Now, I looked upon the faces of my generals, my daughter, all of them awaiting orders on how to crush our enemies.

Never before had I so longed to drop this pretense. To tear off the ring and the glamour that came with it. To turn my back on my plans and let this place fall to ash.

But that was not an option. I would *not* let Amaranth City fall to ruin. I would *not* let the Darkwinter fae claim Midnight for themselves.

I would *not* become someone else's slave.

It was Oona who spoke next, when it was clear that I could not.

"We've received reports of additional Darkwinter

advances through Dead Claw," she said, "though the gargoyles in and around Stone City are keeping some of them at bay. Skirmishes continue on the edges of Blackbone Forest as well. Darkwinter is certainly our main concern at this point, but the other factions are gaining ground. We're also hearing rumors—and yes, I realize rumors are not facts, but they *are* still worth an assessment. There are rumors of increased magickal activity around the borders, suggesting there are other players at work. Other forces we're not yet aware of."

With a deep sigh, I said, "I'm not concerned with a witless army of imps or half-breeds breaking through our defenses at Amaranth, or with wizards playing games at our borders. Darkwinter is and shall remain our primary—"

"My apologies for being tardy, sir." My missing general barged in, finally ready to make an appearance. He was disheveled and out of breath, his eyes wide with fright. He didn't even salute. "If I may—"

"You *may* explain the reason for your lateness, your rudeness, or the despicable state of your appearance," I snapped, "but I will *not* sit here and listen to—"

"We've received a report from the southern outpost," he barreled on, clearly distressed. "A new threat is making its way across the Boiling Glass Sands."

"What new threat?" I scoffed. "None but dragons can

cross that retched landscape, and none of those beasts have been sighted in—"

"Not dragons, sir."

I stood up. Crossed the room. Grabbed a handful of his shirt and pulled him close, my whole body trembling, ready to erupt, eager to find an easy target for the rage the witch continued to inspire within.

In a deadly whisper I said, "If you've come to tell me that Darkwinter armies have not only built ships to sail the un-sailable Sea of Tranquility, but have devised some way to cross the Boiling Glass Sands without liquifying their very bones, I will tear the tongue out of your mouth and gut you where you stand."

"It's not Darkwinter, sir. Not fae at all." He didn't so much as blink at my threat. Simply glared at me, unflinching in his determination to deliver this dire message.

My mouth turned as dry as the obsidian sands beyond the wall.

"Speak," I commanded. "What new devil has set his sights on my realm?"

"*Her* sights, sir," he said grimly. "The intelligence has been corroborated. The Dark Goddess Melantha has found a way to reverse the banishment spell and return to Midnight. And this time, she's brought the Army of the Dead."

There's so much more to come in book 3, Blood and Madness!

In a world plagued by vicious enemies and the darkest of magicks, it's time for Haley and her red-hot monsters to figure out what's worth fighting for... and whose side they're really on.

The whole crew is waiting for you in **Blood and Madness, book three of The Witch's Monsters series!**

Are you a member of our private Facebook group, Sarah Piper's Sassy Witches? Pop in for sneak peeks, cover reveals, exclusive giveaways, book chats, group therapy to deal with these killer cliffhangers, and plenty of complete randomness from your fellow fans! We'd love to see you there.

XOXO
Sarah

LOOKING FOR AUDIOBOOKS?

A New Way to Get Your Audio Fix...

Audiobook lovers, you can now buy audiobooks directly from my author store at **SarahPiperBooks.com/shop** for early access and huge savings!

The books will still be available on other retailers like Audible and Apple, but buying direct means you can:

- **Save big.** Author store prices are 30-60% off retail prices.

- **Be the first to listen.** New releases will be available for direct buy for a limited-time advanced release 2-4 weeks before they hit Audible and Apple. After that, they'll be removed from the author store to comply with Audible's exclusivity rules for 90 days before returning again.

- **Directly support your favorite authors and narrators.** Your support means the world to me, and helps ensure I can continue to partner with the best narrators in the industry to bring these stories to life!

Visit SarahPiperBooks.com/shop to get started!

MORE BOOKS FROM SARAH PIPER!

Looking for more Reverse Harem romance?

THE WITCH'S REBELS is a supernatural reverse harem series featuring five smoldering-hot guys and the kickass witch they'd kill to protect. If you're wondering about Haley's sisters and the Battle for Blackmoon Bay, this is the series where it all begins!

TAROT ACADEMY is a paranormal, university-aged reverse harem academy romance starring four seriously hot mages and one badass witch. Dark prophecies, unique mythology, steamy romance, and plenty of supernatural thrills make this series a must-read!

In the mood for some naughty vampires instead?

Get bitten by the VAMPIRE ROYALS OF NEW YORK!

DARK DECEPTION kicks off Dorian and Charlotte's story, a scorching vampire romance trilogy featuring a dirty-talking vampire king reluctant to take the throne after his father's demise and the seductive thief who might just bring him to ruin... or become his eternal salvation.

HEART OF THORNS is the first in Gabriel and Jacinda's series, a trilogy starring an ice-cold vampire prince and the witch he's captured from his enemy—the only person who can break his family's blood curse. Gabriel is Dorian's youngest brother, and his story picks up right where Dorian's ends.

ABOUT SARAH PIPER

Sarah Piper is a Kindle All-Star winning urban fantasy and paranormal romance author. Through her signature brew of dark magic, heart-pounding suspense, and steamy romance, Sarah promises a sexy, supernatural escape into a world where the magic is real, the monsters are sinfully hot, and the witches always get their magically-ever-afters.

Her recent works include the newly released Vampire Royals of New York series, the Tarot Academy series, and The Witch's Rebels, a fan-favorite reverse harem urban fantasy series readers have dubbed "super sexy," "imaginative and original," "off-the-walls good," and "delightfully wicked in the best ways," a quote Sarah hopes will appear on her tombstone.

Originally from New York, Sarah now makes her home in northern Colorado with her husband (though that changes frequently) (the location, not the husband), where she spends her days sleeping like a vampire and her nights writing books, casting spells, gazing at the moon, playing with her ever-expanding collection of Tarot cards, binge-watching Supernatural (Team Dean!), and obsessing over the best way to brew a cup of tea.

You can find her online at SarahPiperBooks.com, on TikTok at @sarahpiperbooks, and in her Facebook readers group at Sarah Piper's Sassy Witches! If you're sassy, or if you need a little *more* sass in your life, or if you need more Dean Winchester gifs in your life (who doesn't?), come hang out!

Printed in Great Britain
by Amazon

76934455R00180